The Cottage Porch Stories

The
Cottage Porch
Stories

Soul Parables —
A volume of short stories,
inspired by God,
penned by Roschelle.

Library of Congress Control No. 2006937762
ISBN: 978-0-979069-60-4

Rock Dreams Press
P.O. Box 218080
Nashville, Tennessee 37221

All photos © Roschelle Ridenhour except front & back panels of dustjacket.

This is a personal invitation to nestle into your favorite quilt with a cup of tea and take a journey through the lives of others. As the threads from each tale weave a tapestry of the joys and sorrows of life, may it help you to have a better understanding of your own.

Contents

*Thanks to those who encouraged me
to be disciplined and vulnerable.
Dedicated to God for showing me
the best choice is to be brave.*

My Brother's Keeper

*I*AM SHAKING as I open the cab door. Is it because it is sixteen degrees outside or that I am nervous? I read the address to the cab driver. He looks at me as if to say, "Are sure you want to go there?" then shrugs his shoulders and punches the gas. I pull on the skirt of my navy suit and wonder why I dressed the way I did. Slacks would have been more comfortable and appropriate.

In my hand, are two photographs. One is of my brother Holden, the other of my brother Samuel. I am somewhere in Detroit, searching for Holden, a brother whom I haven't seen in years and who may not even be alive. How I got here is too bizarre, especially for a girl who grew up in a small rural town in Iowa, a town with a population of fifteen hundred. This trip would count as one of my big adventures.

As I settle in for the long cab ride, watching the row houses pass by, I recall memories of growing up with Holden.

For the third weekend in a row, I am at my grandma's house. It is about four in the afternoon and my mom will be picking me up anytime. My parents and brother have spent the weekend in Des Moines in a counseling program. I am scared. Last week I overheard my parents talking about my brother, drugs and a group home. I didn't understand it all, but I did understand since my parents and brother fought all the time, they were considering having him living somewhere else, at least for a while.

It is summer so the soda I am drinking is warm. I could have gotten some ice cubes but Grandma didn't fill up the ice trays until earlier today, so they are still water. In the winter, the soda was cold because it would sit on the steps that led down to the basement. However, in the summer, it is different. Only the necessary items that might spoil go into the refrigerator. Grandma claims it takes more electricity and therefore costs money, so she never puts soda in the refrigerator in summer.

I am standing in front of my grandma's off-white refrigerator that she calls an icebox. It is an old one, the kind that is never seen anymore, with a rounded top and a long metal door handle. The freezer is small with thick ice surrounding the interior. It always needs to be defrosted. Inside are two metal ice cube trays and a box of fish sticks.

On the outside of the refrigerator are pictures of children. Most of them are quite dark-skinned and have very few clothes on. For as long as I could remember, my parents' and my grandma's refrigerator have held pictures of children I have never met. "Who is that?" I ask, pointing to one of the children as I swallow the warm root beer from the glass bottle.

"That is your brother" Grandma replies. I laugh. I think Grandma has lost her mind. "Grandma, Holden is my brother and he has blond hair and blue eyes," I say.

"This is your across-the-sea brother," she says.

By that time, my young mind has wandered onto something else and I go into the living room. She quickly follows me, grabs my root beer and briskly makes her way back to the kitchen.

The screen door opens and in steps my mom, just as Grandma came back through the kitchen door, smiling and wiping her hands on her worn apron. Grandma winks at me. "That was a close one," I think. My mom seldom allows me to have soda, candy or chewing gum, especially not so late in the day. Grandma, on the other hand, is a little more flexible and loves to indulge me, without my mom knowing, of course.

I am being reared in a small town, where the differences in days were not many. We go to the local Baptist Church where my mom and dad both sing in the choir and where every Sunday we go to church and Sunday school. On Sunday nights at six, we go to Training Union. I am busy with school activities so long as they do not interfere with church activities.

When I turn ten, I begin paying more attention to the pictures on the refrigerators. In Sunday School, we have been studying countries and the places our church supports mission projects and missionaries.

Realizing there are people in the world who don't have electricity, running water and, sometimes, food makes me more curious than worried. Although I try very hard to imagine life without electricity, clean water, food and other things I took readily for granted, it is difficult to picture such circumstances.

Somewhere between the ages of ten and thirteen, my curiosity turns to compassion. It launches in me a desire to know all the people my family and church has supported through the years. I learn from my parents the reason we did not take many vacations, and why when we do, they are usually camping trips. My parents have chosen to use "vacation" money for missions.

The cab hits a pothole and I am jolted back to reality. In this particular part of Detroit, the houses are becoming more rundown. It begins to rain. I put the pictures into my purse. I am desperate to find both of my brothers, but for very different reasons. Holden has been gone from my life in Iowa for many years. In my mind, it seems, the boy in the picture, smiling and holding a bat and glove doesn't exist anymore.

Holden's communication to my parents was erratic. Over the years he has been in and out of prison. One good thing about his being in prison was that he had a consistent address so Mom and I could actually write him. Prison made him vulnerable and scared so he made contact with us. Mom would take advantage of the months or years and write him. Dad never wrote Holden or read the letters we receive from him.

When Holden was not in prison and would decide to write us, we discovered he had been all over the world. We received postcards from Costa Rica, Venezuela and remote parts of the world. He wouldn't write much sometimes, only "Hi from Holden."

If he called us when he was in the States, we always knew it was Holden. The phone would ring late at night and an operator would ask if we would accept a collect call. And that is how we kept in touch with my brother, or rather the way he chose to communicate with us for years.

Mom kept all Holden's letters in one of my dresser drawers. In another drawer was an accumulation of other letters. They consisted of all the correspondence from my brothers and sisters overseas. I once was so enthralled with missions and third world life that at one time I considered being a missionary, but something always held me back. Instead, I have followed my father's footsteps by going into investment counseling.

I don't know how Holden and I turned out so differently coming from the same family, but we did. Even at a young age, when my bedtime was eight–thirty and his was nine, it was no big deal to me. We were allowed to read, so when it was time to go up to my room, I did. However, my brother always put up a fight. "Why do I have to go to bed when I'm not tired?" he always argued. He tried to negotiate on anything and everything our parents, especially Dad, ever said.

One summer day Holden came home, curiously quiet. Later that evening when my mom was washing his jeans, she found a five–dollar bill. Nowhere could we as kids could have come up with that much money. Apparently, at just the age of nine my brother had figured out what day of the week and what time our neighbor, Mr. Scheel, mowed his lawn. So, my brother had promptly walked up to the front porch, opened the door, walked into Mr. Scheel's bedroom where his wallet lay and taken the cash.

Another time, during the school year, I came home to see my dad, mom and brother all sitting in the living room. This was unusual because my dad didn't get home from the bank until six every night. I was asked to go to my room, but since our house was pretty small and my dad's voice was loud, I overheard everything. My dad was a gentle, quiet man so I don't recall him ever raising his voice much to mom or me. It all would change when he was dealing with Holden, especially this time.

Holden had been caught shoplifting a lighter and cigarettes from our local drugstore. I learned later they were cigarettes because my parents had actually used other words and I didn't know what that meant. The owner, Mr. Charlie, didn't call the police. Instead, he called my dad.

We had known Mr. Charlie as long as I could remember. On most Tuesday nights, our family would go down to Mr. Charlie's drugstore for dinner. On one side of the store was a row of booths, along with a counter. We ordered hot dogs or cheeseburgers, french fries and chocolate malts. It was the only dinner of the week my mom did not prepare and, unlike her meals, didn't reflect the basic food groups.

After the drug store incident, the fighting between my parents and Holden grew more intense. I couldn't tell what was going to happen to my brother. Talking to him, grounding him, going to those weekend counseling sessions—nothing seemed to stop my brother from disobeying and lying to my parents.

I would pour out all my problems to Samuel, my brother in Africa. There wasn't anything Samuel and I couldn't write about. Although I had never met him, he was my best friend. It wouldn't be until much later when I grew up and started asking the right questions, I learned just what kind of physical danger Samuel and his family were in. Some people in his village weren't keen on the idea of Americans sending money or the fact that Samuel's uncle was running for political office.

Holden left home his junior year, a week after his seventeenth birthday and the day after one of his baseball games. My mom and I had been at his game. Two benches held all the players. My brother wasn't sitting with the guys from our youth group who were on the team. Instead he sat with the three or four other guys.

Most of the other guys were from "broken families," my parents called them, and some were known to drink and smoke. What seemed a small thing to most people was a big thing to my parents, things like sitting by the right people and having friends whose parents weren't divorced. We weren't even allowed to go into the local pool hall, which also served food. Even though our pastor went there, we still weren't allowed. I did not go to the local bowling alley until I was out of college.

Such rules seem strange now, though they weren't then. Alcohol was one of the most dreadful sins, according to my parents. We didn't have any in our home. In fact, one time when I was at Janice Lemmon's having dinner; her parents each had a glass of wine. When I went home and told my mom, it was months before I was allowed to go over there to play and I never again was able to accept a dinner invitation.

As I reflect back, my parents were probably too strict on Holden or at least did not understand him. They were just doing what seemed best. What drew me to my parents caused Holden to rebel against them.

I knew the week before, the situation was escalating to a point of no return. On my brother's seventeenth birthday, Mom went into the kitchen to get the cake she had baked and I went upstairs to get the gift I had made. It was a key chain with words that spelled "FAITH."

Before the conflict between my dad and brother became so bad that they weren't speaking, there were fun times. My dad and brother would have some sort of fake wresting match with my dad always pretending to lose. This year was different. My brother sat withdrawn in the chair, tapping his foot and chewing his fingernails, two habits which made my father angry. My father seemed out of sorts. He paced the floor, fumbled the change in his pocket and nervously straightened the drapes.

The next morning there was a note on my brother's unmade bed, telling us he was tired of this boring, conservative and judgmental family. "You won't find me, so don't go looking for me. I am gone forever," the note ended.

I saw him only twice during the next few years. He came to my high school graduation and sat on the opposite side of the gym from my parents. Mom in her hat and white gloves dabbed at her eyes with her white hanky with her initials embroidered in blue. She tried to make her way to him after the ceremony, but he had already left.

The second time was at my parents' funeral. Since my senior year of high school, my parents had gone to a marriage retreat every February. It was their third year of being host counselors. On their way home, a drunk driver hit them and they died instantly.

At their funeral, I found myself looking at Holden and remembering how good he was to me, when I was little. Even when his friends came over, he always let me hang out with them. He also rode the bus with me during my first and second grades. His school was just a few blocks from our house and he was allowed to walk, but he knew how I hated riding the bus. It was scary and loud, so there he sat, next to me on the bus, for two years.

Holden had no interest in the house they had left to us. He stayed only three days, long enough to sign papers and then he was gone, this time going to Detroit. Before he left, he hugged me. As he turned and walked out the door and down the front porch steps, he pulled something out of his pocket. He held up the "FAITH" key chain I made him so many years before. Then he gave me the peace symbol and was gone.

I am praying he is still in Detroit, still at the address written in the corner of this old faded envelope. The cab abruptly stops in front of an old building. All too soon I am standing in front of an old door with 2A lettered on it. I find him. He actually recognizes me more quickly than I recognize him. He is thin and shaven and he is wearing expensive shoes.

In his one–room apartment, we sit on the only two places to sit, except the twin bed mattress that is shoved in one corner of the floor, a flat sheet lying scattered upon it, and a pillow in a brown pillowcase with orange flowers. A worn afghan is wadded up at the end of the bed. We sit on two lawn chairs, the kind with metal arms and plastic weave that is always torn. But there I sit, pouring out my story.

I tell him I received a letter from Samuel a little over three weeks ago. He was attempting to set up a medical practice in a rural area. People in this particular area, like so many, have never had accessible medical assistance. The closest clinic, a three–day journey, has only a nurse on staff. As usual, there is much political upheaval and not everyone welcomed Samuel's presence. He had built a small clinic, but it had been burned to the ground. He then tried to buy a small make-shift building. The letter described in detail all the problems he was encountering and all the hopes and plans he had for this community.

Samuel needed money for a plane ticket for his wife and their baby. He felt it would be best for them to leave there for a few months. He wanted them to come to the United States. Sending Samuel money is one of the most satisfying things I have ever done in my life. It was my parents' support that enabled him to attend college and medical school. Although my parents had supported many children through the years, we had the greatest and longest ties with Samuel. He was truly interested in changing his corner of the world. My family was interested in investing in that mission and vision.

When the money I wired was rejected and Samuel did not contact me, I knew something was wrong.

I stare at my brother. I am grateful he stopped taking drugs, but distraught because he is still very involved in the drug world. He doesn't say that, of course. We go out for a very nice dinner. I surprise my brother by ordering a glass of wine. Although I still feel a twinge of guilt, I have learned occasionally to enjoy a glass. His phone rings throughout the entire meal and sometimes he answers it. The price of my entree is more than I spend on groceries in a week.

Here I sit, having done nothing remotely illegal in my whole life, and now I am trying to get my drug–dealing brother to go to a third–world county to find my other brother and his family and to help them escape whatever trouble they may be in.

I hand Holden an envelope. He opens it and winces when he sees how much cash it contains. He chides me on how foolish it was of me to travel with so much cash.

I fly back to Iowa and try to proceed with my life. I am behind at work, so I stay late, but no matter how much work I do, my mind is always on Africa. More than ever before, my nights seem especially quiet and lonely. I barely eat or sleep. It has been over six weeks since I visited Holden in Detroit. The thought has crossed my mind more than once that Holden may be somewhere enjoying the cash I gave him since, of course, I hadn't heard from him.

Saturday around one in the morning the ringing of the phone pierces the darkness and startles me out of a much–needed sleep. It is Holden. He won't give me details, just says to meet him at the airport next Wednesday.

It is February, the eve of my parent's anniversary death. It is snow-ing heavily and I am hoping there will not be any flight cancellations. But there have been, so instead of Holden's plane getting in at eleven, the arrival has now been postponed until five the next morning.

I greet not only Holden, but the most beautiful baby girl I have ever seen. I swallow hard as I stare at her dark skin and big eyes. Her brown curls make their way down to the tip of her ears, which are pierced with gold earrings. It makes me laugh, because my dad did not allow me to get my ears pierced until I was eighteen.

A very tired Holden hands her to me. Her name is Elizabeth. She is Samuel's daughter. Both Samuel and Elizabeth have American names. Samuel was named in honor of the missionaries who had changed the lives of Samuel's parents. Elizabeth was my grandmother's middle name.

Over the next few days, Holden pieces the picture together. Elizabeth's parents are dead. I cannot believe it. Though it seems impossible for my heart to bear more pain, I have lost someone else I loved.

I don't ask how he was able to get through customs with a child. This is only one of the million questions I need answers to. In the days to follow, I am overwhelmed with the loss of Samuel and his wife, and that loss seems to invite the pain of my parents' death back in. But then I glance over at Elizabeth. She is sitting on a blanket, contently playing with her toys, and I settle down as joy fills my heart.

Holden says he must go. I will never forget sitting in the living room playing with Elizabeth and watching him walk out the door, wondering if we would see him again.

The next summer Holden comes home and for three months, it

is glorious. He loves Elizabeth, he helps around the house, my heart is full of joy, and once again, I have peace. As promptly as Holden showed up, he leaves. I am glad I do not realize what I knew later, that I would never see him again.

It is now Elizabeth's fifth birthday. After cake and ice cream, we get out the book from which we are choosing which overseas child we are going to support. We always add someone new for each birthday. Some people think it is foolish, all the money I am sending overseas but I cannot see it any other way. This is my life calling, my way of serving. The reward of having Elizabeth in my life is the fruit of my planting.

I often think of my brothers, Holden and Samuel and how I lost both of them for two very different reasons.

Place Settings

I AM SITTING in a four–star restaurant in Portland, Oregon. I arrive before my husband Kaleb. We are meeting here on a date, a directive from our marriage counselor. This is the same restaurant where we became engaged over seventeen years ago. My husband is late. His tardiness is one of many frustrations I have with him. I order a glass of wine, and then change my mind and order a bottle, an expensive one. A little passive–aggressive behavior on my part, I admit. We have short–and long–term savings, an emergency fund and money in the bank, but if my husband had been sitting across from me, we would have perhaps ordered a glass instead of a bottle because he is obsessed with saving money.

I am not against saving money. I want to have a healthy view of finances, but spending money is not the end of the world. So, as on many subjects other than money, my husband and I are polarized. By the time Kaleb reached thirty–two, he had actually attained a large percentage of his financial goals. I had been able only to write mine down on paper at that age. This, of course, is one reason I was attracted to my husband so many years ago.

Even though we have separated, he will now have to rectify our budget. Will this bottle of wine be an entertainment expense, dinner expense or personal counseling expense? I smile slyly as I sip my wine.

In our courting years, money seemed to be no problem, which is how we became engaged at this restaurant. Kaleb courted me and indulged me with gifts. He wined and dined me. Then, abruptly after our marriage, the heavy accountability set in. At first, I was relieved that he was taking charge of an area in which I hadn't really earned a gold star, but after years of his inflexibility, along with other personality conflicts, I had had enough. I announced in a vitriolic tone that I was leaving him. He responded by being more shocked than disappointed.

Now, after six months of separation and five months of counseling, we are on an assigned "date night."

The sun has gone down on the glistening water that surrounds the restaurant below. I begin sipping my second glass of wine. I look around. The table next to me is being set. The candle is lit, the crystal glasses and china beautifully placed.

I am suddenly brought back to a random memory of an incident from my childhood. I pour my third glass of wine and relive the story as I wait for Kaleb:

I remember a cool summer day in 1964 late in the afternoon. The aroma from the kitchen made its way to the front porch. I was lazily bouncing a ball, trying to get it high enough to touch the porch ceiling. The excitement of summer break was long over, and the start of the next school year was too many weeks away to anticipate. As I made my way inside to the stove, Mother patted my head. She always sensed when I was restless. I remember many times in the middle of her day, she would stop to play checkers or cards with me, but not today.

I wanted Mother to have one of the family's special dinners. No amount of begging could coax my mother into having dinner in the formal room. 'Not tonight,' she said firmly. I should have known by her tone that today was not going to be a day for special things.

I loved those special dinners. The formal dining room was my favorite place in the world to be. When we dined there, my mother would bring out her beautiful antique dishes on birthdays, holidays or whenever she deemed appropriate. Sometimes the special occasion was scheduled when my sister and I needed 'extra' attention; for instance, when my sister didn't make the cheerleading squad or when I wasn't invited to a classmate's birthday party. These special dinners in the formal room were big productions. Everyone would dress up. My daddy would look so handsome in his Sunday best, with a gold pocket watch in the left pocket of his gray vest. My sister and I were even allowed to wear make-up. We would go into Mother's room to sit at her vanity. The two side drawers held treasures for me. It would take me so long to choose the makeup I wanted. I loved sitting on the small vanity bench, looking at myself in the tri-fold mirror. Though Daddy didn't approve of our wearing makeup, he reluctantly complied, since we never left the house with it on.

Beautiful china would be set on a delicate white linen tablecloth embroidered with roses and huge silver candlesticks would adorn the table. It was the prettiest place on earth. We all had to use our best manners. Daddy would pull out our chairs for us. I felt like a young queen on those occasions. I loved laying the white linen napkin across my lap. My favorite outfit was the one I'd worn on Easter–a navy blue sailor dress with two red anchors embroidered on the collar. I loved my white tights and black patent leather shoes with big buckles. As Daddy dimmed the lights, the candles were lit, making the dishes sparkle like diamonds. Mother looked so beautiful that Daddy would pretend he couldn't breathe and say, "She takes my breath away, she takes my breath away!"

I felt safest sitting at the table with my family and even now, I remember that feeling as vividly as when I was a little girl.

On a warm August day during my fourteenth year, my sister and I were arguing, or having a "fuss" as my mother would say. I don't know why, but it seemed these days everyone was fussing with each other. I could hear my parents' shouts above my sisters. It was so scary, so very scary, when my parents fought, but even when my heart pounded with fear during their fights, I would laugh. They were always arguing about something incredibly stupid through the eyes of a fourteen year old: the trash cans sitting too close to the curb; the neighbors' cars; the unmown lawn; Dad's secretary was too nice; or, how the money Grandma gave us should be spent. The list seemed endless.

This time the fight was about my mother's wanting to drive five hours away to an airport to see a friend who would be delayed there for a few hours. Daddy said it was foolish, that money was tight. It was dangerous for her to go alone. He couldn't take off work, so he wanted us girls to go with her. My mother wanted to go alone to visit her high school friend whom she hadn't seen in years. "I can make the drive by myself," she argued. This was unusual. I cannot remember any other time, my mother ever going anywhere alone.

The adamant red faces, clenched fist, and short answers at dinnertime told me the fight was far from ended. Usually, my mother would have given in before matters went that far.

Around ten that night, Mother came into our room. I quickly wiped my tears on my cotton gown. "Girls, I am going to the airport tomorrow. I will be leaving early in the morning, so I won't be here when you wake up. I will be back about this time tomorrow night. Bella, you do the laundry. Katie, you clean the bathrooms. Don't eat too many snacks. Daddy will take you to the Hamburger Shack for dinner. I love you both." My sister and I were in shock. Never in my fourteen years had I ever seen my mother not acceding to my dad's wishes.

It took me a long time to fall asleep that night so I woke late the next day. I jumped when I saw my daddy sitting at the kitchen table. He was supposed to be at work. I fixed a bowl of cereal and ate it slowly. He drank his coffee, ate his toast and read the paper. He ended up going in later.

It was the longest day of my life.

I heard a noise around midnight so I crept out of my room. I pulled my t-shirt over my knees and peeked over the banister. I was shocked to see my daddy setting the table in the formal dining room. He smoothed out the tablecloth, gently setting the plates, only two of them on the table. I will never know what he put on those plates since I had never seen my daddy cook. I heard my mother pull into the carport. I watched as she slowly closed the screen door, pulled the key quietly from the lock and walked over to the formal room, probably to see why the light was on.

My mother witnessed for the first time in their marriage the table set without her help. In the middle of the table were four dozen roses. It was plain to see mother was deeply shocked. Daddy was a thrifty man. He may have "borrowed" a few roses from our neighbor and given them to mother occasionally, but "I've never paid for a flower," he would proudly boast. As I saw tears welling in my mother's eyes, I felt the sting of my own tears. She and Daddy did not say a word. He walked over to her gently and, it seemed, a little fearfully and held out his hand. She did not move. He moved closer and took her into his arms. They seemed to hold each other forever. They didn't eat or sit. They just stood there. I was soon bored and went to bed.

The next morning, after Daddy had gone to work, Mother fixed us cinnamon pancakes. There was a strange expression on her face all day.

Things changed around our house after that. I cannot really figure out what happened, but now Mother never nags Daddy about the lawn, and he has a new secretary at work.

The dishes stayed on the table in the formal dining room for three days before Mother cleared them. When she did clear them, she made Katie and me go help our neighbor Mabel pull weeds in her garden. She did that when she wanted to be alone.

Kaleb arrives, he kisses me lightly on the forehead and picks up the bottle of wine as he sits down. When the waiter comes to the table, Kaleb requests another bottle. He gently takes my hands, and we look deep into each other's eyes as tears drop into the empty china plate sitting before me.

The Christmas Tree Farm

I CELEBRATED my seventy–first birthday today. I had a wonderful day, beginning that morning with the ringing of the doorbell. Of course, no one was there, just a basketful of muffins wrapped carefully in a very old blue and yellow checked dish-towel. The "birthday basket" was a tradition my dear friends initiated years ago. We take turns preparing a breakfast treat for one another's birthday. It seems silly, but we just cannot stop doing it.

For lunch, Bettie, Tilly and Blanche take me to a quaint tearoom. We eat too much, laugh loudly and talk at length. After lunch, there's a drive to my favorite park where we take a walk. The jonquils are in bloom, reminding us spring is on its way.

Later in the evening Campbell and I go dancing. Afterwards, we share a huge piece of chocolate cake with hot fudge sauce, fresh rasp-berries adorning the side of the etched glass plate. After a pleasant evening, Campbell takes me home. As he rounds the car to open my door, he tries to secretly retrieve a gift from the back seat. He walks me to my door and hands me the gift; I smile. He knows I won't open it until I am alone. He kisses me on the cheek, walks back to his car, then drives home to Dottie. Dottie, his wife of fifty–nine years and my best friend.

Dottie is sitting exactly where Campbell left her. He thanks the nurse and rolls Dottie's wheelchair into the kitchen, getting out her nightly medicines. After twenty minutes of sipping water and swal-lowing pills, they go to the back deck. It has been their nightly routine for years, to go outside before bed and enjoy the night sky. He has continued that routine even though he isn't sure why.

There is a chill in the air, so he tucks the lap blanket in tightly around her small thin frame. The sky is beautiful and full of stars. Campbell talks about his night with Anastasia but trails off into si-lence as they both sit. He takes her hand and smiles, making their way back inside to get ready for bed.

I sit down on the sofa, getting ready to pull the bow off my gift that Campbell brought me, when the phone rings. My son is calling from Africa to give birthday greetings to his "best girl." After the call, I return to my present. I unwrap the picture and smile. It is a picture of me. I have long forgotten the year, but I know when I turn over the picture there will be a note with a story.

I look long at the picture. I am standing among the trees. I have on a very old pair of corduroys and a red flannel shirt. I smile and hold the picture close to me. I will wait until tomorrow to read the note and story.

Anastasia. I had hated my name for so many years, and would insist people call me Andie, but Campbell and Ashton refused. They said I was royalty and always called me Anastasia. For so many years I would fall asleep with Ashton whispering, "Good night, my dearest Anastasia." Dottie's real name had been Dorthalea and, just like me, she didn't like her name.

Campbell and I had kissed once. It was about a year after Dottie's stroke and years after Ashton's death. It was on my birthday and we were both lonely. We were very dear friends but we each only had one true love. So we held each other for a long time but knew friendship, a very treasured friendship, would be the only thing between us. With Ashton being gone and Dottie no longer mentally with us, all we had was one another, it seemed.

For forty years, Ashton and I had owned a Christmas tree farm. I was twenty-four when I first stepped foot on the "Branson Tree Farm." I had recently moved to this small town and decided, for the first time in my life, to get a real tree for Christmas. I had thrown on some sweats, kicked my way through many unopened boxes scattered on the floor, and headed out the door.

At the farm, I soon realized I was in over my head. The trees were all shapes and sizes. I didn't know which one to pick. So, when the most handsome man I had ever seen offered to assist me, I consented. Not only did Ashton Branson help me pick out a tree, he also took it to my house in his truck because it wouldn't fit into my small hatchback. I hadn't considered how to bring my tree home. He stayed and helped me decorate it. The next night there was a knock at my door. There stood Ashton with mistletoe. Six months later we were married.

We ran the Christmas tree farm for several years with Ashton's parents and then upon their retirement, bought it from them. We met Campbell and Dottie during the first Christmas we owned the farm. They were last in line for hot chocolate, but we had run out. Ashton and I invited them to join us at our house up the road. The four of us talked and laughed for over two hours. It was the beginning of a nurturing friendship.

For the past twenty–five years, we two couples had lived a few miles from one another. When Ashton died, I could hardly bear losing him. Campbell and Dottie helped me survive my wrenching loss. I stayed with them that first week after Ashton's death. Every morning I woke to find Dottie, wrapped in an afghan, asleep in the corner chair. Soon the desire to be in my home with Ashton's things in it, gave me the courage to return there.

Almost three years have passed since Dottie had her stroke. Her illness took us all by surprise. Now she is almost incapacitated. Campbell brings in a nurse just a few hours a day to get out of the house. He takes a walk, usually to come check on me.

Since Dottie's stroke, I have taken dinner over to Campbell and Dottie every Tuesday and Friday night. Campbell and I still talk and laugh, but we miss Ashton, Dottie, and all the memories we had.

Campbell and I will play cards just as the four of us had done for so many years, but it isn't the same.

I sit on the chair in the corner of the bedroom. It has been six months since Dottie has been gone. Campbell decided it's time to go through Dottie's belongings, so we have spent the last few days sorting through things, deciding what to keep and what to throw away.

We are down to one dresser in the guest bedroom and the hall closet. Campbell takes the closet. In the bottom drawer, I come across an old gray wool pullover sweater, a rock, a man's watch and a large worn brown envelope. I toss the rock in the trash but then something makes me take it back out. It then hits me, first the sweater, Ashton's sweater. Campbell had gotten it for Christmas one year but he was allergic to wool, so he gave it to Ashton. Ashton had worn it for years. One day the four of us were hiking and Dottie had gotten cold. Ashton gave it to Dottie. Why had she kept it?

I am confused, and then something starts slowly sinking in. I open up the brown envelope. It is full of letters, tied in two bundles. I recognize Ashton's handwriting on the envelope. I take a deep breath and unfold one of the letters. Before I can read it, I lay it face down on my lap. My stomach churns. I twist the wedding band I still wear. Campbell yells from the stairs that he is making his way downstairs to fix lunch.

I pick up the rock and the memory returns. The four of us are on another hiking trip. Ashton had found the rock and was smitten by it for some reason. I turn over the letter and begin to read the words on the yellowing paper. When I finish, I crumple it up and toss it into the blue plastic trashcan. I read some more of the letters that my beloved Ashton had written, not only to another woman, but also to my best friend. I fish the letter from the trashcan, lest Campbell finds it. I hear the phone ring and am relieved. Campbell will be delayed in making lunch. I slip both bundles, tied with a brown shoelace, into my purse.

I go into the bathroom. Draped over the gold towel ring is a worn powder blue hand towel with the words "Welcome, Friends" embroidered on it. I grab it and pat my eyes, then splash my face with cold water. I stare into the mirror. I take the three wooden stairs leading downstairs rather slowly. I walk past the living room and into the kitchen. Campbell looks up and smiles. He pours me some iced tea, finishes peeling an orange and sets half of it on my plate, the other half on his.

I take a bite of the tuna sandwich. "Did you find anything in the dresser drawers worth saving?" Campbell asks.

I smile at him, pat his hand, swallow hard and say "Nothing worth keeping."

Grandmother's Hatpins

I SETTLED on a navy blue hat, with a price tag of one hundred and fifty dollars. It is extravagant, I know, but Grandmother is worth it. It fit her perfectly, she looks beautiful. I turn to go great the guests that have arrived at the funeral parlor.

Today, I buried my grandmother. She was also my mentor, mother, father and closest confidante. In her ninety–six years, I had never heard her complain. I was going to miss her terribly, her example and influence. Grandmother Gertie raised me and sacrificed more than I ever have had to in my life. As I ride back from the graveyard, I silently reminisce over tidbits of her life.

Gertrude Lamel Mason was her name. Most folks called her Gertie. She was a loving and patient woman most of the time. She did have a few strict rules: no feet on the furniture, no shoes in the living room and no one was to touch her hats.

Most of my memories of my Grandmother are warm and loving. She had gentle eyes and a tender smile and always made me feel I was the most important person in the world. When I was young, one of my favorite things to do was to act out plays. She would sit there amongst the few dolls and stuffed animals and pretend to be enthralled with all the hoopla. She would comment on how talented and witty I was and would applaud loud and long.

Looking back now, I don't know how she reared me alone. Maybe because she had no choice? When I was two, my momma had left me with Grandmother for a Saturday afternoon and never returned. I never met my dad. He'd left before I was born.

Growing up, I was energetic and Grandmother seemed to do everything in slow motion. Whenever I pestered her to hurry, she would say, "Patience, Betsy, patience!" If I bothered her too much, she would make me spell patience. I think I knew how to spell that word before I could spell my own name. Once during my third year of school, I had to write out the word "patience" one hundred times.

I remember one Sunday when Grandmother was taking her dear sweet time getting ready. She was a simple woman and usually didn't make much of a fuss over her appearance. Sundays were different. She always put on a dab of perfume and a little make–up. Grandmother took the longest time choosing a hat. She wanted to make sure she had picked the best hat for the dress she had chosen to wear.

It was interesting to watch Grandmother select a hat. She got the same expression on her face that she had when she was buying fruit and vegetables at the farmer's market. She wanted to make the best choice. Today I was "seemingly so impatient," she said, so I tried not to leap off her bed when she was ready for church.

My grandmother always looked beautiful sitting in the wooden church pew. She sat so straight and proper in our pew as if she were a queen. She listened intently to the preacher. I was always looking around, watching the ladies, seeing what they were wearing, who got their husbands to church this time and who didn't. When I was little, the church seemed so big. It seated only about two hundred people, but for me it was a big world.

Grandmother had rituals. Friday nights we went shopping. Saturdays were for chores and on Saturday nights we rested. Sundays were my social time. I loved Sunday school and church. Usually, we would go to someone's home for lunch, or on a few occasions, hosted a family in our home. Of course, I preferred to go to the homes of someone who had children. However, I would make do if they didn't. I would sit among the adults, talking only when asked a question, taking everything in, feeling privileged that I was with the "grown–ups."

One particular rainy Saturday when Grandmother Gertie couldn't think of another chore to do, she resorted to reading and tried to persuade me to do the same. Soon she was sleeping and I was restless. I sneaked up to her room. At the time it seemed the thing to do. I slowly opened the old wooden closet door and jumped as the door creaked. I peered into the small closet. On either side were two small horizontal poles that held clothes. Straight ahead were three small shelves. They held my Grandmother's hats. There were two hat boxes on the floor full of hankies and gloves.

I soon was trying on all the hats, turning them to one side, then to another. I'd leave the closet and go to the back of the bedroom door that held a full–length mirror. I had the hats all scattered about when it happened. I don't know how, but one of the hatpins stuck into the side of my finger and slid down, ripping my skin. I screamed into my shirt. I was bleeding and blood seemed to be going everywhere. As I ran out of the closet, somehow I smashed my bleeding finger in the door.

My finger throbbing mercilessly, I ran to the bathroom where I haphazardly wrapped the bleeding finger in a tissue. It hurt and I was crying. It seemed as if I stayed in the bathroom for hours.

At dinner, I pretended nothing happened. Grandmother was shocked when I turned down dessert and asked to be excused early to go to bed. I woke in the middle of the night with my finger throbbing and swollen. I went into the bathroom looking for some medicine and the light woke Grandmother. She opened the door and when I saw her kind, tender expression on her face, I began crying and showed her my finger.

She fixed my finger right up and it seemed to stop hurting. Then she asked how I'd hurt myself. I tearfully told her the story and she sent me to bed. Years later I discovered she knew all along what I had done because of the evidence I'd left in the closet. I had stepped on some hats and torn them. Blood had gotten on her white Easter hat.

Two hats were wedged in the door, and when she pulled the door open, they ripped.

The next day seemed to be the longest Sunday in my life. We still went to lunch as planned but I just couldn't really enjoy myself, and Grandmother wasn't saying much.

When we got home, Grandmother sent me to my room. I didn't know what she was going to do. Only twice before in my seven years could I remember her even being angry with me. Thinking of it now brings a smile to my face, but it didn't then.

The first time we were in the kitchen making apple pie for some important person coming to visit our church, I had for the third time stuck my finger in the cinnamon and sugar mix after being asked twice not to. She took the metal spoon with which she was stirring the apples and whacked it across my hand twice. I think it startled Grandma as much as me, that she had hit me so hard. The bruise stayed on my hand for three days.

My second misdeed occurred at church. I was tired of sitting and the sermon was boring. I decided to wiggle around so I could see my friend Darcy on the other side of the church. Grandmother gently nudged me and I turned around and sat up straight for a while, but soon I had twisted around again. This time she pulled me closer to her. Now, I don't know what got into me but I decided to turn around again, and as I did, the heel of my black patent leather shoe hit the knee of Charlie Kinkead, the gentleman sitting next to me. He flinched and his foot kicked the pew in front of him so hard the communion glass fell out of the holder and onto the wooden floor, where it broke into three pieces. Grandmother pinched my arm so hard I let out a yelp. As further punishment, I spent the next two Saturdays at Charlie Kinkead's home raking leaves in his yard.

However, this time it was a spanking. I cried. Grandmother had never spanked me before. I stayed in my room the rest of the day.

It took years for me to realize how poor we were. We went to people's homes on Sundays for dinner because our church family knew that most of the time, we didn't have a lot of food in our house. That explained why we never had many people over. I remember that on many summer nights during supper, Grandmother would say, "Child, it is just too hot for me to eat." I didn't realize it then but it was because we didn't have enough food for the both of us.

It wasn't until I was in high school that I learned my grandmother had scoured the "back roads" for many of our clothes and house wares. In our little town, the wealthier people had an unwritten pact among themselves. On the third Thursday of each month, anything and everything they no longer wanted or needed was taken out to their back porch, back yard or the street behind their homes. Anyone could walk around the neighborhoods choosing items they needed: clothing, hats, dishes, towels, toasters, rugs, blankets and many other things discarded. After I came to live with Grandmother, this is what she did, she had no choice.

Of course, I didn't know any of this until I was much older with a career and a family. Sometimes on our Sunday afternoon drives when Grandmother was very old, she would tell little stories about those difficult times. Nor did I know those dabs of perfume were really vanilla water. On the next Mother's Day after I heard the vanilla water story, Grandmother Gertie received ten of the most expensive perfumes the department stores had in stock. When I visited her a few weeks after that May Sunday, she had only two bottles. She had given eight of the bottles away to her friends, but she certainly enjoyed the perfume she kept. She would almost gag us when we picked her up and took her to church with us. She would get into the car, smelling like a perfume factory, but we never criticized her for it. It made us smile.

"Is Grandma Gertie in Heaven?" my young granddaughter Annabelle asks. I pull her up onto my lap. Everyone else is in the house, eating. Annabelle and I were sitting in the swing on the front porch. She smiles, revealing two missing front teeth as I assure her Grandmother Gertie is in heaven. She takes my hands and wraps her little ones around them. She studies my hands and fingers and wants to know about the scar on my finger.

As I look down at the scar on my third finger, a half–inch scar from a hat pin that earned the only spanking I had ever gotten from my grandmother. I say, "Oh, Grandmother's hatpins, Grandmother's hatpins!"

Aunt Mattie's Journal

PING! PING! PING! Rocks hit the side of Mattie's truck. It is actually a loud thud, the rocks are large. But Cort's hearing had gone bad years ago, although he would never admit it. With each rock thrown towards the old truck, Cort grew angrier and angrier. A cold rain was coming down in sheets. Cort was drunk and oblivious to the fact. Since he was not a drinker, it didn't take much to put him into a state of intoxication. "Mattie, come back. I demand you to come back now! Please, God, do something! I cannot take this. I refuse!" Cort screamed maniacally. His words did not stop there. His expletives filled the silent night air. If anyone had seen Cort, they would have either laughed or been shocked. Cort was ordinarily a quiet man who rarely showed his emotions. He hadn't always been that way. He had once been kind, gentle, and attentive. All that changed on the day his son died. In his mind, it was "the day I killed my son." He had always felt responsible for Jacob's death. Mattie tried to convince him he was wrong, but to no avail.

Although his arms were weary, his gray hair drenched, Cort continued to throw rocks. The glass from Mattie's truck windows were sprinkled on the ground. Cort's feet were bleeding little teardrops of blood. The alcohol had prevented him from realizing the cuts or pain. The thunder was loud, seemingly trying to drown out Cort D. Lawson's cries. It was only later, much later, he realized it was three in the morning and he had been outside in the rain far too long.

Cort stumbled up the porch steps, not realizing he had had the same t–shirt on for days. He pushed open the front door. It resisted. Trash was piled up inside so high he could barely get through. His stomach growled profusely. He did not remember what or when he ate last. Out of character, he picked up a blanket and tossed it onto the sofa.

The bright sun woke him from his stupor. He rolled off the oversized, brown sofa and the pain struck him. Looking down at his feet, he realized he had stepped on some glass. When? Where? He lay back down, his head and feet throbbing. The room was spinning. Cort fell asleep again.

When he woke, he stumbled through the cluttered living room. Mattie's blue sweater was still draped across the rocker. Mail from weeks past was scattered about on the ottoman. He walked to the bathroom to nurse his feet. It was the first time in weeks he had tried to do something to help himself. He fearfully looked into the mirror. Although his feet were aching, he rested his hands on the basin and stared into the mirror. He was dirty and his hollow eyes made him flinch. He slammed his fist on the basin, and began to cry. He missed Mattie. If only she could see him now, crying like a baby. The last time she had seen him cry was the day their son Jacob died, so many years ago. He had now outlived his wife and son. This brought only bitterness to his heart.

For the first time, he realized how messy the house had gotten. At least two months had gone by since Mattie passed away. He had neither showered nor washed a dish since the day after her funeral.

He'd had plenty of company the week before the funeral. Mattie had been taken to the hospital late one Sunday afternoon. Mattie had awakened not feeling well and returned from church early, clearly a sign to Cort that she was ill. She passed out in the hallway before the ambulance arrived.

During those few days in the hospital, she did not open her eyes for Cort. She woke only once. Sophie, Mattie's niece was the only one in the room at the time. Mattie had called out, "I am going to be with Jacob soon, real soon."

And that is how it ended; Mattie's brain aneurysm had taken her life. Sophie, was the first to come and the last to go. She didn't want to leave, but Cort insisted that she go back to Boston.

Sitting on the sofa with some bandages from the bathroom, he picked glass out of his feet. It was painful and took a long time. The living room was filled with pictures. He went to one of the walls and took down a picture of Mattie. She was standing in the garden in well–worn jeans, her hair tied up with a red bandana. She had an incredible smile and there was a smudge of dirt on her left cheek.

It was one of Cort's favorite pictures. He threw it across the room. The dark spot on the wall stood out. Cort walked over to the now–cracked picture and hung it back. Pictures of Jacob lined the other wall. Cort inspected each one. He then found himself at the end of the staircase. His fist came down hard on the rail and pain seared his hand.

He made his way into the bathroom and, after having a shower, he made his way to the kitchen. The refrigerator contained only spoiled food. In the cupboard, he found a can of tuna and a can of tomato soup. He opened them quickly as he was profusely hungry. It was the first time he'd felt like eating in weeks and, after eating the tuna and soup, he opened another can of soup. Looking around the house, he realized how much it was in disarray. The living room was the worst. He didn't know where to begin. He had never been much of a housekeeper that had been Mattie's department.

He tried to close the drawer on the wooden coffee table. It was stuffed with papers and wouldn't close. He opened it and took some of the papers out. Still, the door would not close. He reached behind the drawer and realized something was caught. He loosened the stack of papers and closed the drawer. He started to take the stack of papers to the trash. When he realized there were a few notebooks in the pile, he stopped, gasped slightly and sat down again.

In his hands were a few of Mattie's journals. He knew she had kept notes for years. She was always writing something down in their bedroom, kitchen, laundry room. The journals had never really interested him before. But now, did he dare read them? What would he find?

Enraged, he threw them into the trash. He ran through the house, going into all the rooms, throwing open drawers, letting Mattie's clothes fall everywhere. By the time he had finished, the messy house looked even worse. The kitchen trashcan overflowed with numerous journals. Other types of journals decorated the floor below. Cort kicked the trashcan and the small amount left in the can of tomato soup spilled onto the floor.

The next day Cort took the journals from the trash. He wiped them off as he set them on the gray Formica table. Sitting down, he began to decipher the piles of journals. Some dated back to high school days; some had no dates. Two caught his eye. They were titled "Dear Jacob" and "Alone." Cort took a deep breath. He couldn't handle it. He stared at the journals for over an hour without opening any of them. "I can't take it," he told himself and he cleaned the living room, watered the slumping plants, and straightened the rug. He then found himself back at the table. He read through them randomly. He opened some of them in the middle. In some of them, he looked only at the last page.

He spent the next thirty-two hours at the table, drinking black coffee and reading. He couldn't have slept even if he had wanted to.

When he finally made it outside, he noticed the damage to Mattie's truck. It looked stripped. The dents were beyond repair. "Who did this?" he hollered. Had the storm caused the damage? Then he realized he was the vandal. He had thrown the rocks, he had destroyed the truck. It all came back to him. In a drunken stupor, he had destroyed Mattie's pride and joy.

He reflected on the time she had bought the truck. He'd thought she needed a car; she'd wanted a truck. He had begrudgingly bought it, lecturing her all the way home. Through the years when anything was wrong with it, he would whip out the lecture as if he had just written it. Cort knew she would never trade it and never admit defeat. Mattie had a love affair with the truck and with life.

Cort hated the truck. He had handed her a large sum of cash one day, saying to her, "Go buy a new car or truck, anything!" She refused. "Why did I not scoop her up in my arms?" he asked himself. He smiled when he thought of her now, her stubborn little face with the turned–up nose. She was right; the truck had been a good buy. She had invested wisely, made a good choice. "Mattie, come back," he ashamedly whispered and mentally replayed her journal notes:

....December, 1928–We buried Jacob today.

....July, 1929–Cort sold the family farm, and we moved eight hundred miles from you. It is beautiful here. You would have loved it, Jacob. Cort was gone all day and came back with gallons of blackberries and wildflowers. I made pies all afternoon.

In the background, he heard the answering machine. "Uncle Cort, please pick up your phone. If you don't call us, we are going to have to come check on you. I know you don't want visitors, so please call me." It was Sophie's third message, which, she knew, would go unreturned.

....December, 1932–I went back, I had to, and visited your grave. It has been four years. I miss you desperately. I planted some flowers. Jacob, I wish your father would come but I can't get him to. Why do my tears flow so easily? Your dad never cries and he is cold and distant. He won't talk about you. Have I lost him too?

....September, 1944–I visited your grave today, Jacob. It has been sixteen years. You would be twenty-five today. I bet you would be as handsome as your father was when he was your age. I cannot get him to come with me. He still won't talk about you. He wants to pretend you didn't exist, and I want to pretend you never died.

....October, 1944–I can remember before Jacob's death how happy we were. Cort had so much of life to live and love to give. How could one day make it all vanish? The love was buried with Jacob. Dearest Jacob....When you were born, your dad had a difficult time going to work. He was such a hard worker, but he would give anything to spend another minute with you. He started taking you with him to the fields at age three. You were much too young and I thought it would be too much for you, but you went. You dreaded lunchtime because you knew you would stay behind for a nap and your dad would go back and have fun without you. I can still see you, standing by the screen door, your chubby little hands waving long after your dad's tractor disappeared around the barn and over the hill.

Your dad would read to you in the big rocker by the fireplace and rock you to sleep. It wasn't until you turned six and the both of you couldn't fit into the rocker that you would finally would hear bedtime stories from your bed.

....December 1946–I remember the morning of your death. You and Cort were going sleigh riding. You were nine years old and when your dad and I woke up at six-thirty, you were already awake and dressed. Today was the day to try out a new route. You had discovered it while hunting. You and Cort were waiting for a good snow so you could try it out. You returned to me, folded up like a rag doll in your dad's arms. After your funeral, I watched your dad take the sled, or what was left of it, along with your blood-soaked overalls and coat, and burn them. He sat by the fire for hours, throwing on logs and cursing into the night sky.

....August, 1949–Today was a beautiful day. The sunshine warmed my soul. I took bread to Flossie. I fear she won't be with us much longer. My heart is heavy. I want my husband back, the one who died alongside Jacob. Does Cort love me anymore? Does he not see behind the gray wisp of hair and the faded apron there is a woman who wants to be grabbed up and taken outside just to get a glimpse of a bright moon. To be danced with, made love to on the cold linoleum floor or outside on a fall afternoon? I don't want him to just touch me, I want him to feel me.

....August, 1954–Today the flowers are blooming and I decided to take a long walk. I don't know why, but I couldn't stop crying. I know it is silly, but I just keep thinking I might get pregnant. Yes, it would be foolish at my age. I keep thinking about Jacob. We had tried to have other children, but I wasn't able. Maybe we should have adopted. Maybe we should have been foster parents. Cort would never talk about it much. Maybe I should have insisted. I am just a little weepy today because it is the end of summer. I have seen all my nieces and nephews over the summer. Each came for a week at a time. It was so much fun and so rewarding. Since your death, Jacob, they have brought such joy into my life. They don't replace you, but they help ease the pain.

He gathered up the journals. After he showered, he pressed his best shirt and polished his shoes. As Cort left his home of so many years, he pressed his cheek against the apron that hung on the hook by the kitchen door. He breathed in Mattie's fragrance for the last time.

Sophie receives a package, in a scribbled hand writing, on a piece of yellowed paper, "Your Aunt Mattie would want you to have these."

The town folks were surprised to hear the news. Cort Lawson's house had burned to the ground. Cort's body had been found hundreds of miles from home. He was found in a cemetery, lying beside a grave. It was Jacob's.

The Price You Pay

*T*HERE IS A COST to everything, a price, a sowing and reaping. I have counted the cost, but am I ready to pay it? I think of Lillian Somerset. I think of the prayer journal I found that she kept in the later part of her life. She paid the price. I don't remember Lillian. Oh, I do when I glance at the pictures of her and me. She spent a lot of time with me when I was about three until the age of six or seven. It was mostly in the summers when I would stay with my grandparents, Opal and Ephraim Jones. Did she really see my call so clearly? According to her prayer journal she did. I don't know how my story ends but I do know how Lillian's did. So, I tell it to you. I close now because, if I am going to get the best deal for that overseas flight, I have to book it today.

Lillian Somerset chose to take a mission trip to gain a break from all the practical book application she had received over the years. Her parents and professors urged her to go straight into the Master's program, but didn't win out. This journey, though, was for only eight months, a short–term mission trip to a remote village in a third–world country. She would return in July and begin her Master's program in August. She had traveled many times and loved the adventurous flutter in her heart when she headed for the international flight sign at the airport.

She knew the flight would be long. She came prepared with books to read, letters to write and an assortment of crossword puzzles, but nothing could hold her interest. Instead, she flipped restlessly through the magazines the airline provided.

Upon her arrival, the missionary couple, Sam and Jo, with whom she had been corresponding, greeted her. She instantly fell in love with both of them. Sam had a strong handshake and a shiny baldhead. Jo's hug and smile told Lillian she had found a friend for life.

Lillian was tired. The four–hour bumpy road from the airport caused her whole body to ache. She had heard about the roads there, or lack thereof. Her mouth was dry and her feet hot. Her first day was supposed to be spent unpacking. Instead, she attended the funeral of a young boy. Little did Lillian know it would not be her last. Lillian soon learned that the villagers burned all the bodies. She could expect nothing less in a community lacking water and electricity, where disease and death ran as rampant as did the children.

Their work was exhausting, yet was the most rewarding thing she had ever done. There were many needs, so they went out each day to the villages and returned each night to their little hut. She ended each day feeling blessed to be there, but in the same thought, counting down the days until departure. Part of the problem was her inability to sleep. It seemed she would doze off and fall into a heavy sleep, but then wake up in a fitful state.

Three months passed and she still had not slept through the night. If she were in the States, caffeine or sugar too late at night could have been the problem, but those things were not accessible here.

The days turned into weeks. One morning, Lillian's day began, as usual, by getting water. She felt uneasy and restless, but cast it off as another night without good rest. She carried with her a watering can and some rice and bread. She rounded the small turn in the road as she had done many times, but something stopped her. Tired, she decided to sit under a nearby tree for a moment. She realized she must have dozed off because voices awoke her. Before she could get to her feet, she was hit on the head. It all happened in a split second. The last thing Lillian remembered was her hand pulling the bark off the tree.

When she woke, something was wrong; Lillian did not try to move but continued to lie in the dirt. She felt lightheaded and nauseated. Her head was aching and there was blood, but not from her head. Her clothes were ripped. She realized she had been raped and a wave of grief washed over her. She attempted to stand up, but fell down and passed out again.

Much later, Sam and Jo found her. They had become worried when Lillian hadn't returned by sundown. It was a solemn walk home. It was the longest, darkest night of Lillian's life.

The next day they went to a makeshift police station, no hospital or clinic: there wasn't any nearby. The small, smelly room was lined with cracked plastic chairs. They sat for over two hours watching the small room fill up. By that time, it was sweltering in the crowded room and the sounds of crying children on the street seemed to permeate the conversations going on inside. A large police officer finally arrived, barely fitting through the narrow door. As he walked through the room, he spit tobacco, which landed on an elderly woman's arm.

Lillian wanted to leave, but the policy of the United States mission program with whom she worked required her to file a report. She mechanically signed the numerous forms. It seemed so surreal. After talking with the police officer, she learned it would take months to go through the process. The government was indifferent. They were in no hurry and were apparently unconcerned about finding the man or men who did this to Lillian.

Being an American in this third–world country was not the most popular position in which to be. Yes, there were many needs there, but the local governments did not look favorably on anyone coming in to change the system, even if that change might bring clean drinking water, education and hope. At that point, she did not care. She just wanted to go home, not to the hut, but to the United States. She kept this to herself.

After a long day, they returned to their huts. The next day, as in many days that followed, she refused to go to the villages with Sam and Jo. She rarely talked to them when they returned. Instead, she spent her time trying to get a flight back to the United States.

She wrote letters and tried to make arrangements. She wanted to go home—now!

Weeks after the rape, Lillian was preparing a light lunch when the room began spinning and she vomited. She sat down, weeping. Lillian knew before her body displayed the sign, she was with child. In a flat tone, she told Sam and Jo.

Lillian was enraged. She was out in the wilderness with miles and miles of open land, but felt smothered and caged. She told Sam and Jo that after she had the baby, she would return to the States, alone.

The months passed quickly. Lillian's stomach grew. One night in her seventh month, a sharp pain woke her. She arose quickly from her bed and noticed blood. Sam and Jo were aware of the danger. The doctor was not scheduled to be there for six more weeks. They all knew there were no medical services nearby. "Take this child, God. If you love me, take this child!" Lillian screamed. Sharp pains racked her body. They all looked at one another, realizing Lillian was in labor.

Fifteen hours later, Sam laid a newborn son into Lillian's arms. Lillian refused to look at him. "I don't want to touch him!" she screamed. They left the room. She consented to nurse him. If she didn't, the child would starve.

With the passage of days, Lillian found herself falling in love with her son. He was restless when she was not holding him. At times, though, she was still angry, her heart still enraged, and nothing seemed to make sense. He was beautiful and Lillian could not help but to be quieted by his presence.

One night as Lillian sat outside enjoying how the full moon lit up the sky, she made a decision. She would not go back to the States. She also decided on a name for her son—Gabriel. After that, Lillian had no trouble sleeping through the night.

Gabriel grew quickly and the years passed in the same manner. He was handsome and strong. There was an energy and a spirit of rebellion about him. Perhaps rebellion was too strong a word; it was more the absence of fear. Lillian realized if his energy was not channeled towards the vision and needs of the surrounding villages, it would be to his detriment. At age five, he announced he would become a police officer and work for God. Lillian smiled and told him he would change his mind a million times before deciding, but he looked her in the eye and said, "God said so, Mom." And so the years passed.

The government was cracking down on foreigners, especially Americans. Officials had become more inquisitive and wary of outsiders. Most of the time Sam, Jo and Lillian were left alone and not interrogated. They had brought productive farming initiatives and cleaner water, along with techniques to help eliminate disease, so most of the officials tended to leave them alone. In addition, Sam and Jo were quite respected in the community after living there so many years. They had begun by not being allowed to teach the children. Now they were not only able to teach the boys, but also girls, and even some of the women. Sam and Jo had been there over thirty years, Lillian eighteen. They had seen so much change resulting from the fruit of their labors. Although they were grateful for the physical changes they had made, the underground churches were by far the most valuable and rewarding project they had accomplished.

Gabriel joined the local police, miles away from the small hut he lived in all his life. For the next ten years, he was relentless. With his position and the holes in the system, he was able to smuggle forbidden literature into this third–world country, literature that influenced and changed so many lives.

It happened quickly one night. Sam felt uneasy all day and dismissed the study group early. Sam, Jo, and Lillian were walking along the dusty makeshift path lit by the bright moon and a small flashlight Sam was holding. They were stopped in their tracks by five police officers. The men startled Sam. He tripped. The flashlight bounced to the ground. When Sam picked it up, the light shined directly on Gabriel.

As Lillian looked at Gabriel, she realized the danger more than ever before. Yes, she knew people were consigned to prison for spreading the gospel. Yes, they had to be careful, but somehow now it was all too close. Her insides began to shake and her heart pounded.

In all those years, how could she have been oblivious to the danger that was now staring her in the face? If she had chosen not to face it, would it have taken her back to safety? The lead police officer walked over to Sam and pointed a gun directly at Sam's temple. Without forethought, he looked at Gabriel and gave the order, "Take this man to the field." Gabriel and Sam walked slowly to the field. Jo and Lillian joined hands. Not one–half mile away in a field laid four pastors praying fervently for their leaders.

Sam turned and looked Gabriel squarely in the eye. "You must kill me. It will further the gospel. The underground church will grow. This is God's way." Gabriel began weeping, and Sam opened his arms to Heaven.

In a second, it was over. Jo and Lillian stood, frozen. They wept. The police officers moved away as quickly as they had appeared. Gabriel did not look back at Jo and Lillian.

A few days later, Lillian woke early with the same unsettled thoughts she felt on the day she was raped so many years earlier. All too soon, her uneasiness was confirmed. Confronted by two police officers, she was commanded to gather her few belongings and go with them. Where was she going? She asked to see Gabriel, but her request was denied. She begged them to tell her something about her son. Jo stood in the small hut door watching the police officers take Lillian away. If Lillian and Jo had known this would be the last time they would see each other, it might have been too much to bear.

She learned later that officials were suspicious about Gabriel and had been tracking him for a year. Her request to see her son was again turned down. Instead, a short man driving a small rusted car with a loud muffler took Lillian to the airport. During the drive, Lillian stared at the ticket and two hundred dollars a police officer had shoved in her hand. Through no choice of her own, Lillian was flying back to the States, her life threatened if she ever tried to return.

She felt anger again, deep raging helpless anger, such as she felt after the rape. She tried to let it subside. She closed her eyes and tried to sleep. Then a sensation like fire ripped through her. Lillian jolted up and out of her seat. She knew then as she knew the time she was pregnant—the truth. Lillian laid her head back on the headrest and began to weep. Her anguish was indescribable. Gabriel was dead.

All of a sudden, she became nauseated and in a whisper cried, "No, please God, do not let me vomit." The man by whom they had seated her had been very quiet and seemed annoyed by her presence. She did not want to disturb him. However, it was too late. She vomited on the empty seat between them.

A very kind attendant helped her to the bathroom. She cried out to God with questions. Her parents were dead and she had no siblings. What would she do when she arrived there? What was happening to Jo?

When she stepped out of the bathroom, the attendant moved her to a different seat next to a young man whose long hair covered the headphones, but not the loud music coming from them.

Halfway through the flight, after dozing off and on, she realized the young man had taken off his headphones and was turned towards her. They introduced themselves. Creighton Jones was a student returning from an overseas vacation, a college graduation gift from his parents. He asked where Lillian was going. She told him she wasn't sure, that it was a long story. He seemed genuinely interested, and after he asked a second time, Lillian decided to tell Creighton the whole story. She needed to talk, to let out some of the pain. Before another word left her mouth, her heart's burdens seemed to be lifted.

When she finished, Creighton gently reached for her hand. "You are coming home with me." Of course, Lillian politely declined, although she didn't know why. Creighton persisted. His parents lived in Maine on thirty sprawling acres and ran a small publishing company. Creighton's grandmother had passed away recently, leaving the small guest cottage empty. Lillian finally conceded at least to go with him until she could get her thoughts together and decide what her next step in life would be.

Lillian Somerset lived to be over one–hundred years old, having spent the remainder of her life in Maine with the Jones family. She spent her time tending to the gardens, sitting on her front porch watching sunsets, and working with her local missions group at church. Her letters to Jo and surrounding contacts were never answered. She died never hearing from Jo or knowing what happened to her.

Until of course, when she got to Heaven, united with all of her family where she learned Jo had witnessed to and brought three of the four police officers to the Lord before the fourth one shot her. Those three police officers launched over forty churches, bringing the gospel to more unreached people than anyone had done before their time.

My Ancestor's Cabinet

I OWN A SMALL bed and breakfast in Kentucky. It is open Thursdays through Sundays, April through October. I bought it in my seventh year of private practice as a counselor. So now a few years later, I am able to practice as a counselor and run my bed and breakfast. The bed and breakfast is a great diversion from my counseling world. I like both jobs; they require different strengths, keeping me balanced.

It is Wednesday afternoon. My last two appointments canceled at the last minute, so I am taking advantage of the time. I rush out to the mall. I am looking for some pajamas. I make my way in and out of stores. I cannot seem to find what I am looking for.

I am tiring of the mall, all the choices, the crowds, the teenagers, the babies, the aggressive salespeople or, the opposite fact, that now I cannot find anyone to help me.

Holding pajamas, I walk towards a salesperson and from the corner of my eye, I see robes on sale. I make my way towards them. All of a sudden, my eyes latch on to a bright pink robe. I become dizzy and short of breath. I take a step back, try to take a deep breath, and try to close my eyes for a couple of minutes. None of those strategies work, so the pajamas are deposited on a table nearby and I quickly exit the store.

It now seems hot and terribly loud in the mall. People walk by me swiftly. I make my way to a bench. It is crowded, but they reluctantly make room for me.

Sitting on it are an old man and a hefty young girl eating a doughnut while trying to quiet a crying baby. I don't want to sit there but I know I cannot make it to the car, nor do I have the ability to look around and find a different bench.

The memories are searing the corner of my mind. Mom's pink housecoat, worn thin at the elbows, a safety pin holding the ripped pocket on. There is a two–inch rip in the back where the housecoat was caught on a nail. As with most memories, I cannot think about my years growing up without thinking about the house in which most of those years were spent.

Of course, when I think of my house, I instantly think of the kitchen. The walls were painted yellow, with the exception of one, which was bright blue. It seems the painters had run out of yellow paint and left it blue. On that wall hung a cloth calendar with brown buttons, a picture of a green teapot and the words "Happy New Year" in gold lettering. A stained red–checkered tablecloth, full of holes, covered the wobbly, old table. In the middle of the table was a dirty, tan, Lazy Susan.

On the Lazy Susan was a layer of grime, which kept a pair of salt and pepper shakers in place. They were glass with a black "P" on one and a black "S" on the other. A syrup lid with a dead fly lay next to it. The glass vinegar bottle was half–full, and the outside was covered with fingerprints.

As I would spin the Lazy Susan around and wait for breakfast, I wished for normal food. Sometimes it would be, but I can remember many mornings when it wasn't: cereal with orange juice instead of milk, waffles with heated jelly, or toast with syrup. I always ate whatever was set before me. It was good that we had food to prepare. There were many times we didn't.

Looking back, I think that I was so happy my mom was attempting to care for me that I would have eaten anything. I was not sure what it was like for most families, but growing up I knew something was wrong in my home. I was certain not everyone had a home like mine. While my mom made me breakfast, she would drink.

When I left for school, she kissed me goodbye with a mixture of cigarette and alcohol breath as she held the door open for me. She would diligently watch me get on the bus, waving until the bus was out of sight.

Once on the bus I would shrink into the nearest seat and open my lunch box. Sometimes there would be a sandwich, chips and if it was a good day, maybe an apple or carrots. Other times there would be random foods: ketchup and pickles, an egg, a bag of pasta noodles, a box of prunes or worse, nothing.

I learned never to bring anyone home after school. I had once and it didn't go well. My friend cut her finger and we went to the medicine cabinet to get a bandage. Of course, there were no bandages, only bottles of alcohol. It didn't surprise me, alcohol was everywhere in my house. My little friend was scared. She did not know what they were or why my mom was sleeping in the middle of the day. She began crying and ran out of the house and down the street toward her house only a few blocks away.

Growing up I was very lonely, but it helped to have my brother there until he ran away. He and my mom did not seem to like one another. He ran away at the age of twelve. I was in third grade. Years later, when living with my relatives, I learned he was not even my brother.

I am calming down. The mall doesn't seem to be as loud, the people don't seem to be walking as fast, and I am not sweating anymore, but I can't make myself stand up. "Abigail Renee, snap out of it!" I tell myself, but self-talk just isn't working, so I choose to process some more of my memories of our home and my mom. I am trying to practice what I preach. I am quickly brought to the upstairs hallway, especially the closet.

It was a small closet with two shelves. On the top shelf was an old vaporizer, a board game of some kind with half of the pieces missing, a blanket and mismatched sheets. The second shelf held our towels. Most of them were old and ragged; sometimes they would rip when I was drying off. We never threw them away; we merely cut them into smaller squares and used them as washcloths.

An oblong vacuum cleaner sat on the closet floor, its cord frayed and most of the attachments either broken or missing the piece that would keep it attached to the vacuum. The bottom of the closet also held an assortment of alcohol. One time I counted twenty bottles.

It seemed that there was alcohol behind any cabinet door we opened in our house. In our kitchen cabinets, we may not have been able to find food but we could always find alcohol.

At times people would leave food on our front porch. At Thanksgiving and Christmas, we would get ham or turkey. I was always so happy then. There would be a whole bag of food containing potatoes, cranberries, pumpkin pie and bread. Usually, the baskets came from the local church down the street. On one Thanksgiving, I had no idea how to fix a turkey, but I was hungry and my mom was passed out on the couch. I couldn't read very well but I followed the directions. It wasn't ready to eat until ten o'clock that night, with my mom long gone to a bar with a current boyfriend. I ate the whole thing: the turkey, the potatoes, the dressing. It all tasted wonderful.

I am not sure why my mother drank. I just know that when I came home from school, I would wake her up. I might find her on the sofa, the television blaring loudly; other times she could be in her bedroom or even on the kitchen floor. I would wake her up and she'd stumble to the bathroom and take a shower. She would prepare dinner while I did my homework. She never helped me with my homework, but she expected decent grades. She would sit at the table after dinner and smoke cigarettes while I tried my best to clean the dishes of the day. The breakfast plates and anything else mom had used that day would still be where they were left. While I washed dishes, she would look as if she were trying to review my schoolwork.

Afterwards Mom would go upstairs and get ready. Most of the time I'd follow her up to her room and sit on the bed as she put her make–up on. The music would be blaring and a film of cigarette smoke would linger in the air. Sometimes she would grab me and we'd dance around the room with her hugging me and patting my head. It was then, when I knew my mom was getting ready to leave for the night, that I missed my brother the most.

About nine o'clock my mom would tuck me in and kiss me with her painted lips. After I heard her car leave from the driveway, I would go downstairs and make sure she had locked the door. Ever since my brother had left, I was scared. I would go through the house checking every window to make sure they were closed, and peeping out to see if anything or anyone was out there. I would sit on the couch with its springs poking through the brown material and watch television. I always kept the lights off, afraid someone would know I was by myself. I was always thinking I heard noises of some kind outside. I would try to bury myself deep into the couch.

When the news came on, I'd make my way to my room. The news scared me. In my young mind, it seemed it was always about bad things happening. I would lock myself in my room shaking, sure the noise I had heard earlier was now inside my house, not just outside the window.

It seemed anyone I cared for somehow left. First, it was my brother, and then the Spencers. I threw up three days in a row before they moved. They left on a Saturday morning. I sat on the swing on their front porch as I watched box after box being taken out and loaded into a big moving truck. After their departure, I stayed on their porch. I remember being cold and hungry but I didn't move. I just knew that if I sat there long enough I would see them come around the block and pull back into their driveway. Coming back, for me.

The Spencer's moved away the summer of my fourteenth year. Mrs. Spencer sewed buttons on my clothes. She was the one who would have gifts at Christmas for me. It was in their living room that I celebrated my birthdays. Every year I would start panicking a week before my birthday, wondering if they would forget and then I would have to go to school and say that I didn't get anything for my birthday. But the balloons would magically appear the morning of my birthday, tied on the post that held up their small front porch. I knew that I would have a cake and presents after my mom had left for the night.

During my senior year, my mother was dying and nothing could prevent it. Most of the year was spent either taking her to the hospital or bringing her home. On the night of my high school graduation, my mother opened up a small wooden box, one I had never seen before. It had the addresses and phone numbers of her sisters. I didn't even know I had aunts. My mom made me vow that I would not contact them until after she had passed away.

On graduation night, I stepped onto the stage and received my diploma. There was no flash from my family's camera, no happy parents standing up and applauding. I went by myself and I returned by myself. I was hoping but not really expecting the Stone family to be there.

Their daughter Toni had been my dearest friend in high school. Toni had been killed in February. She was driving home from the library, slid off the road, down an embankment and hit a tree. Just two weeks before that tragic event, we had received our acceptance letters to college. I knew it would be very painful for them to attend but I certainly wanted them to be there. They had taken me in as part of their family. It was Mrs. Stone who helped me fill out my applications for college and helped me apply for college scholarships and loans. They didn't have much money but since my freshman year when they went clothes shopping for Toni, they included me. I don't think I could have survived high school without them.

On the way home from the graduation, I stopped by the grocery store. There was one cake left in the fresh baked section, a white cake with chocolate icing. I bought it along with a tube of pink icing. I took it home and wrote on it, "Way To Go" cut the cake and ate it. All the while, my mother slept upstairs.

My mother died without admitting she had done anything wrong or saying she was sorry. At her funeral I met my relatives. They remembered me, but I had no recollection of them. I had three aunts. They were kind, generous and warm. The afternoon of my mother's funeral, my new family and I went back to my house. I packed the very few items that were worth taking. I closed the front door, stepped off the sagging porch with the peeling paint on the wooden post. A dead plant in a cracked plastic pot sat in the corner. Once in the car I did not look back.

On the long ride, I learned about my family. I was born in the small town where most of my mom's family still resides. Mom was pretty wild, rebelling against her family and their values. The only thing that my aunts knew about my father is that he had not come to their high school until his senior year. It was only he and his mother. Soon after he and my mom ran away, his mom moved away. She and my father were only eighteen when she got pregnant. Apparently, soon after they moved, and before the marriage could take place, my father left my mom.

My mom found a boyfriend soon afterwards. He and his son moved in with her, but within months, the boyfriend was arrested for stealing and was sent to prison.

I laid my head back and closed my eyes. The car smelled new but my Aunt Hazel assured me that it was an older car. This car was not old; I could tell her about old cars. All the cars my mom ever drove were loud, wouldn't start on real cold days, had torn seats, and it seemed that each one contained a busted or cracked window covered with cardboard and tape.

They decided for the summer I would live with my Aunt Hazel. She had been recently widowed so it seemed the best choice. Slowly, throughout that summer, I pieced together the puzzle of my life. Hearing stories of my family history that could explain some of my mother's choices and behavior.

Learning about her and finally finding a way to forgive her. Although I wouldn't trade my life, I wouldn't wish my childhood on anyone.

My head seems to have stopped spinning. The noise in the mall appeared quieter. I go back into the store and make my purchase. I drive home. I call a friend and then take a long, hot bath and dry off with a large, fluffy towel.

Afterwards, I make myself a cup of tea and sit in front of the fireplace. I have on my new pajamas. I sit there for hours tossing pieces of a new pink robe into the fire.

Ms. Martha

MARTHA JANE SAMSON was born in Louisville, Kentucky, and had resigned herself to the fact that she would die there before her thirtieth birthday. Martha Jane was a plain woman with a small muscular frame. She had drab brown hair and big brown eyes. Along the right side of her eye was a three-inch scar. Her father had hit her with a piece of wood when she was seven. Her mother died when she was eight, leaving behind a scared, timid girl at the mercy of an angry father. With each passing year, her hard life seemed to grow weaker, without promise.

Her wedding, her sixteenth birthday and the final time she would see her father happened on the same day. Having found a new wife who did not want Martha around, he forced Martha into a marriage to a man she didn't know, who would turn out to be a mean man, a very mean man. Martha had believed no one in the world could be as bad as her father, but in the days and months to come, her husband would prove her wrong.

Ms. Martha lived to be ninety. She was buried under a tall oak, which had weathered as many storms as she. So some crisp fall day maybe you will walk by an old weathered oak and think of Ms. Martha Jane Samson. Maybe you will draw hope and courage to take another breath and press on. Here is her story:

She awoke at three in the morning to the taste of dried blood in her mouth. Her hair was matted and stuck to the yellowing linoleum floor. She moved ever so slightly, a trait learned in these last eight years of marriage. She never knew how sore she would be, so the more slowly she moved, the less pain there was. He had started bullying her around six the night before, so it seemed she had been unconscious most of the night. Moonlight poured through the window above the kitchen sink. She closed her eyes and soon dozed off again.

When she next awoke, it was dawn. She sat up too quickly and then lay back down on the cold floor to control the dizziness. Her eyes roamed from the ceiling down to the cracks of paint on the wall to the worn wooden cabinets. The cabinets held only a few items, most of them cracked or broken. She knew she could not lie there long because he would soon be up, expecting breakfast.

Two posts supported the overlay from the counter. Two shelves wobbled between the posts. Her grandmother's soup bowl sat on the bottom shelf and two cookbooks on the second. Underneath the corner of the overlay, something caught her eye. It looked as if there was a box of some sort fastened underneath.

She closed her eyes one more time before she got up. Slowly she stood up, walked over to the sink, and splashed her face with cold water. As she did, she cringed with pain. Her left arm was bruised from her wrist to her shoulder.

She served his breakfast. As on so many other mornings she stood by dutifully as he ate. She didn't have permission to leave the kitchen when he was eating in case he wanted his coffee cup refilled. He finished his breakfast and slurped his coffee. As he got up, he grabbed her arms. She reeled from the searing pain, but she dared not react. He glared at her, said nothing, then abruptly turned and left the room.

She began to tremble and she sank into the nearest chair. As soon as she heard his truck leave, she fixed herself a cup of coffee and made her way outside to the back step to watch as autumn slowly made its way to their part of the country. She took in a breath of the cool, crisp air and even in all her pain, smiled. Fall was her favorite time of year. She glanced over her list of chores for the day. He made such a list every day for her. The lists were difficult to read since he couldn't spell or write well.

She wiped her hands on her apron. The small gas station calendar on the wall read September nineteenth, nineteen hundred and fifty two. There weren't any shelters to call or any neighbors she could ask for help. Once and only once, had she mentioned his abuse to a church going woman. The lady had promptly dismissed her words, saying abruptly, "No man would ever do that to a woman. Why would you make up such a story? Stop making trouble for yourself."

It was almost noon when she remembered the box. Although he wouldn't be home for hours, she peeked out the kitchen window. And when she saw no one, she walked over to the cookbooks and ran her hand underneath the counter. It was too painful to bend. She fumbled nervously. The box was nailed, but the nail was loose. The box slid out and she placed it on the counter. She wiped her hands once again on her apron and peeped out the kitchen window.

Inside the small wooden box was an old tin container. It was rusty, but she managed to get it open. Inside the tin were a sealed envelope and a yellowed piece of paper tied with a length of string. When Martha pulled on the string, it broke. Inside the folded paper were two fifty-dollar bills.

Martha had never seen so much money in her life. She wondered if it was real. She set the money down and opened the sealed envelope. She dumped the contents, a gold bracelet and three rings, onto the table.

She sat for almost two hours, shaking. She was too scared to try on the rings, so she just looked at them. They were beautiful. She had never had much jewelry in her life. When her mother died, Martha was given her jewelry, which consisted of a brooch and a small beaded bracelet. Both pieces of jewelry, her husband had lost in poker games, as most things of value they once owned had been.

Finally, she decided to be brave. She slipped the rings on her thin fingers. She studied the rings. Although they were beautiful to her,

Martha had no idea how much they were worth. Unbeknownst to Martha, she had in her possession an emerald, a topaz and a diamond solitaire ring. Martha wondered who had left them. Would they be coming back for them?

Martha was so caught up in the presence of the jewelry, she almost missed the folded piece of paper tucked up inside the lid. The paper, old and worn, looked as if it would crumble if she so much as touched it, but it didn't as she slowly opened it.

The note was written in the prettiest handwriting she had ever seen. Martha's own writing was messy. She had been allowed to go to school only until the sixth grade. Although she still had her school books and tried to practice writing, her penmanship hadn't improved in all these years. On the paper, most of the writing was faded out, but she made out the words, "Train #35 departure, going to Saint Louis, on to Kansas City." She got out an old map from a drawer to see if she could figure out where Saint Louis and Kansas City were located.

She returned everything to its place and looked nervously around the room as if he were watching her or that he might walk in at any moment. He came home later than usual, though, carrying some groceries. He must have won some money playing cards because they did not have money for food. At least that was what he had told her that morning.

She prepared dinner. Afterwards, he told her to rub his shoulders, so for well over an hour she did, although her left arm still ached from the night before. He finally fell asleep, but she could not. She looked out the bedroom window, watching the elm and oak trees, their limbs swaying but not breaking against the blowing winds.

— 91 —

It took her a few days to get up the courage to ask. She was so scared she felt sick to her stomach, but she asked anyway. Martha wanted to go to town next week with him and spend the day at the library. He had finally realized a few years ago that the more she learned, the bigger the harvest of crops would be and the better she cooked, so he allowed her on occasion to go with him to town and check out books. He, on the other hand, found no use for the library.

She cooked him a piece of cornbread cake and sat quietly waiting for him to hand her the empty plate. She asked him if he wanted more. He nodded and she filled his plate. Later he came into the kitchen and startled her. He kissed her hard, then grinned when he told her to go to bed.

It was a Saturday, and, like most Saturdays of her married life, it was the day she worked on the farm with him. He had rented this small farm with its four acres before he had married her. They started early and ended after dark, plowing, planting, mending fences, bailing hay, butchering hogs. The list was endless and varied depending on the season.

On Sundays, they fished. She was grateful because at least she could sit down. Sometimes they would drive a long time to find new ponds. She would yearn to fall asleep on the drive, but she was not allowed.

On the following Monday, he took her to the library, which was actually four shelves located at the end of the small post office. She had to wait almost two hours before it opened, so she sat nervously on the side of the steps. He took her by surprise and gave her a dollar for some coffee and a sandwich at the local diner. She was glad because she had wrapped up a sandwich and a pickle but had left them behind on the kitchen counter.

At the library, she scanned information about Saint Louis and Kansas City. She had once been told she had a cousin living in Kansas City. She checked out her books from the library. Ms. Martha felt bad about stealing the three library books. She tried to leave the lady a dollar, but the librarian refused, so Martha just smiled as she wrote the date of when the books were to be returned, knowing they never would be.

Martha nervously made her way over to the train station. It was loud and busy and although her husband worked far away from the train station, her stomach churned. She expected him to be around the next corner waiting for her, fearful that he might have figured out her plan.

From the comfort and safety of the railcar, she tried to settle in. She took small bites of a cracker she had gotten at the diner, in hopes of settling her stomach. "Miss, someone is trying to get your attention," said the man behind her. Martha tried to ignore him and kept her eyes fixed on the seat in front of her. "Miss," he said more loudly as he touched her shoulder. "There is a man, look out the window, he is trying to get your attention." She looked down. She could see hatred in his eyes. He was shaking his fist as he ran alongside the train. Thankfully, the train started moving and he was slowly fading out of sight.

She closed her eyes and pressed herself into the seat, hoping to disappear. Only when the train had made its way past the trees, did Martha open her eyes.

She went to the bathroom and vomited up the crackers, the only thing she had eaten in the last twenty-four hours. After splashing cold water on her face, she looked into the mirror. The cut above her left eye had almost healed. She smoothed her hair and made her way back to her seat. She drew the old tan sweater more tightly around her small frame. She could have laid her head against the window to try to sleep, but she was afraid that she would wake up to find him at the window yelling and shaking his fist. She nervously slid her hand down around her sock just to make sure the money was still there. Of course, it was.

After a long nap, she stepped off the train. She was in Saint Louis, Missouri. She slowly made her way through the station. She was trying to find a phone to locate her cousin, when the girl caught her eye. She could not have been much older than sixteen. She huddled in a chair. Martha had never been brave or confident enough to talk to strangers but she walked right over to this one.

It was there she left the first ring, a ring for the girl to escape. Although Martha didn't know the story, she knew those eyes, eyes that tell a story no one wants to hear or believe.

Martha stepped outside, watched the people, and looked around. She carefully made her way across the street. She stayed in the store for over an hour. She looked at things, the threads, the candy and the colored socks, again and again. She had been in very few stores in her life, so she was savoring the experience. She purchased her very first store-bought dress. It had tiny, purple flowers on it and a lace collar. She bought two pairs of white socks because the colored ones cost a quarter more. She also bought a lilac sweater with large white buttons and big pockets.

At the counter, she nervously laid the clothes into the hands of the merchant. She hoped he would talk slowly enough for her to give him the right amount of money and be able to count and make sure she got the correct change back. At the counter sat a small heart shaped necklace in a pink case. She wanted it, but the price of two dollars and ninety-eight cents seemed too high, so she chose two sticks of peppermint instead.

In an abandoned gas station bathroom, she casually tossed her old tan sweater into the trash. Before she could even get out the door, anger took over. She grabbed the sweater from the can and tried to tear it, slapping it against the concrete wall as she screamed and cried. She clutched the cold sink and noticed the rust stains around the drain. She slid down the rough concrete wall between the sink and trash can. As she sat on the musty floor, she sobbed into the tan sweater, screamed one more time, and then fell asleep.

Even lying on the cold concrete floor, she woke only twice in the night, once to the sound of squealing automobile tires and later because two cats were fighting. She slept more soundly than any other night she could remember. Once when Martha woke up, she smiled. She had forgotten just how many pairs of underwear she had put on before she left home that day. She couldn't pack anything, so she had put on as many pairs of underwear as she could, along with wearing two bras. She realized just how uncomfortable she was.

In the morning she wiped her face and once again threw the tan sweater into the trash, but this time was the last. Then she walked out the door.

By the time Martha reached her seventieth birthday, she had been a cook for many, many summers. This camp had been a perfect fit for Martha. She enjoyed the kids, the counselors and the general hubbub that a daily life of camp brings. Another summer session had ended. She had already said goodbye to the campers and now she was seeing the last group of counselors off. She hugged Carrie and Claire and stuck book money into their pockets for their second year of college.

Although the camp was closed until next spring Martha would stay, as always. She survived the long hard winters because to her nothing was hard. She would work around camp most days and read before retiring for the night. She devoured books and learned to knit and crochet. The local dime store had a wide assortment of yarn. She would never buy anything tan. Only the brightest colors would do. Every camper the following summer would go home with something: a hat, mittens or a scarf.

She never found that cousin in Kansas City. She recollected it could have been Corpus Kristi, not Kansas City. She just couldn't quite remember and it didn't really matter. She had her camp family.

Martha at eighty-four traded the second ring in for a burial plot two miles down the road from camp in a local church cemetery, under a large oak tree. They buried her there in the fall of her ninetieth year. Ms. Martha now rests from weariness and work.

Years later, after Ms. Martha passed away and the camp had long been closed, I, Brandy Adams, found myself hiding there. My belly had grown too large to hide, my breasts protruding from the suddenly too small t–shirt. My parents had kicked me out of the house the moment I confessed I was pregnant. The last time I saw my boyfriend, the father of my child, he was kissing the girl who just started working at our local diner.

I slept three nights at the camp before discovering a wooden box underneath the mattress of one of the camp beds. Inside lay a ring along with Ms. Martha's story written out on a tablet of paper. Many years have passed and although I never made much money in my life, I always manage every year to make a donation to my local library in memory of a friend I never met, Ms. Martha Jane Samson.

Winter's Lane

I WAS BORN in rural Connecticut to Radford and Opal Roberson. Until I was sixteen, my small–town life revolved around school, church, and the family farm. The three–hundred–acre farm had been in my father's family for three generations. Life, for me, was safe and familiar, but that was to change all too soon.

When I wasn't in school or at a church event, I could probably be found with my dad. Dad was quiet, patient and hardworking. He worked long days on the farm, partly because his main goal in life was to provide a college education for his only child. I loved being outside working with him. As I look back, it would have been easier if I would have been a boy or if my parents had been able to have more children.

I am sure I held him up on some of the farm chores that required more strength than I was capable of. However, if my father was disappointed about not having a son, I never knew it.

Besides working on the farm, every Saturday night my mom and I would bake desserts for Sunday dinner. Every Sunday after church, we always had a family or two over for dinner, along with Mr. Vanhorn, that is. Mr. Vanhorn owned the farm across the road from us. His family had owned over six hundred acres. He had sold all of it except the thirty surrounding the house. We shared vegetables from each other's gardens and there wasn't a day I didn't see him at least once or twice. We were separated by only a small dirt road. On the rare occasions Mom and Dad had to go somewhere, I would stay with Mr. Vanhorn.

On a warm Saturday night in May, Mom and I were making desserts for the next day. I was very excited. Mr. Vanhorn's daughter, Chloe, along with her two sons, were coming to live with him. Chloe's husband had committed suicide. I wasn't supposed to know that but I had overheard my mom and dad talking one night. He had been a prominent tax attorney in New York who had been caught doing something illegal. Apparently he didn't leave them any money so Chloe and her two sons, Carson and Beck, were moving back here for a while.

I was so happy there were going to be kids my age around, even if they were boys. I would have preferred at least one girl. I had longed to have a sister. I had friends at school but living so far out in the country I didn't get to see them much except at school.

The next day, after church I met Ms. Chloe, Carson and Beck. They were the cutest boys I had ever met which really wasn't saying much since I didn't know many people outside my small town world. We sat around the family dining room table, Mr. Vanhorn seemingly relieved to have us around. Mom and Chloe caught up on each other's lives. They had gone to school together, but as soon as Chloe turned eighteen, she had left. She had returned infrequently; it had been over six years since they had last seen each other.

Carson, the youngest, was funny, energetic and slightly taller than Beck. Beck was quiet and, most of the time, seemed irritated with Carson and me. Carson, in the few months they had been there, adjusted well to farm life. He loved being outdoors and helping his grandfather with whatever chore was needed so, we had a lot in common. Beck, on the other hand, hated all the quiet, and the boring life he thought farm life offered. He said he was leaving as soon as he turned eighteen, if not sooner.

Carson, Beck and I spent our summer evening's together, mostly on my porch and front yard, talking, catching grasshoppers, and playing catch. Beck would be on the porch swing carelessly throwing a ball up in the air, seemingly counting the days before he could leave.

Some nights Carson would kiss me goodnight, just on the cheek, which only left me wondering what it would be like if Beck would do the same. Then I would watch them open up our old iron gate, cross the road and go inside. There were nights that I couldn't sleep and I would look outside. I would see Beck, leaning up against an old Rambler car that sat on the side of his grandfather's barn. He would be smoking a cigarette, blowing rings into the wind. I always wanted to go to him, to comfort him somehow, to sit beside him. I never did.

One night we were sitting out on the wagon, next to the barn, listening to the frogs and staring up into the sky. Beck was trying to pick a fight with Carson, saying cruel things and pushing him. Finally, when Carson pushed back, Beck took a swing at him. I jumped up and ran to Beck, pushing my small arms against his chest. "Stop, Beck, you big bully, don't hurt Carson!" I screamed.

"Why, Leah, do you love Carson, do you want him to be your boyfriend?"

"Beck, you are a jerk!" I said.

Beck grabbed my arms and laughed. He got close to my face as if he were going to kiss me, but I wiggled out of his arms.

Summer turned into fall and school started. At school, Carson and I hung out. He mixed easily with the kids. Beck stayed mostly to himself or around the flock of girls that would follow him. It was apparent that Beck was the best looking and coolest person who ever walked down our high school halls.

Fall quickly turned to winter. After dinner and homework, Carson would come over. He and my dad would talk or we would all play a board game. Beck would come sometimes. I was always disappointed when he didn't and always mad at myself for feeling that way.

We had a few days left of winter break when we had a big snow. Carson, Beck and I decided to go sledding. We were going to take Mr. Vanhorn's old truck around our farm, pulling an old hood from a car with a cable wire.

Mom gave us plenty of hot chocolate and blankets, since the old truck didn't have much of a heater. It was cold and bright. The road had only the tracks from my dad's truck that had gone out earlier that day. It was white as far as we could see. Carson was driving first, Beck on the hood hollering at Carson to go faster. It was fun. We were laughing, freezing, and daring one another to go just a little bit faster, all the while holding on as best we could so we wouldn't slide off the hood and across the snow. It was getting close to dark when we decided we were tired and hungry. Beck was driving and I was sitting in the middle. Carson decided he wanted to go for one more sleigh ride, so he lay on the hood, grabbing onto the edge, smiling and giving me a wave and a thumbs–up. Beck gunned the old truck and we were off.

"Faster Beck, faster," Carson hollered. But then Beck started to slide. He lost control of the truck. The hood was now going back and forth so fast. Carson screamed, "Slow down!" When the hood swung too far to the right, the cable wire broke and flung Carson off the hood, slamming and smashing his body into a tree. Carson's blood scattered across the white snow.

A week after the funeral, Mom came into my room, "Leah, why don't you try to go to school today?" I didn't. I couldn't. I waited two more days. In the weeks that followed, Beck would hardly talk to me. I would sit outside on the porch, waiting for him to open his front door, cross the road, and open our iron gate, but he didn't. For months, I would pass him in the hall at school, he would look the other way.

On a warm night in June, I couldn't sleep so I grabbed a book and slipped out to the porch, only in my cotton gown. I jumped as I saw Beck standing at the end of the sidewalk, leaning against the old iron gate, chewing on a piece of straw. I folded my arms and held the book across my chest, feeling my heart beat against the book. He walked slowly towards me, and then passed me by to the porch swing where Carson and I had sat many nights watching Beck tap the wooden floor with his well–worn boot.

He sat in his sleeveless tee and his muscular arms stretched along-side the back of the swing. I stood there, not knowing what to do. Then I walked over to him and sat down next to him. He pulled me closer. I laid my head on his shoulder as naturally as if I had done it a hundred times before. Beck wrapped his arms around me.

He cried, apologizing repeatedly for killing Carson. I tried to tell him that it was an accident. We sat there for another hour in silence, except for Beck's sobs. Then he reached for me and kissed me. And then I made a mistake, a choice. One that would cause me a lifetime of regret. I wouldn't know that then. The next morning when I got up, I learned that Beck was gone.

No one had heard from Beck in the two months he had been gone. I was getting ready to begin my senior year. We were at the doc-tor's office since I had the flu for a few days. My mom and I sat in silence in the small examining room. I stared at the cotton balls in the jar and tried to count them as we learned together that I didn't have the flu.

My parents decided that I would go live with my grandmother, where I would have the baby and finish high school. I didn't have any choice or say in the matter. In fact, there wasn't much said at all around my house since I had returned from the doctor. My dad hadn't spoken to me since Mom had told him I was pregnant. He wouldn't even go with us to the bus station to see me off. The man who had saved his money to send me to college, who had made a special seat on his tractor, who had taught me how to fish and shoot a gun, would not look me in the eye or hug me goodbye.

I was a junior in college, when, in October, I received a letter from Mom, asking me if I would come home over the Christmas break. Although I struggled and was angry, I longed to go home. There hadn't been a day that I hadn't thought about Beck, Carson and Carson Leann, the little girl that I had given birth to and had given up for adoption.

I arrived home on December 23. Nothing had changed in the familiar house and I could feel the tears creeping up in my eyes. I could hear the television on in the den. Some things never change, my Dad watching the evening news. I looked at Mom, grimaced and walked into the den. My "Hi, Dad," came out nervously and loudly. He put his pipe down and looked up. He smiled, shuffled his papers and slowly got out of the recliner. He hugged me.

That night for dinner we had lentil soup, homemade bread and gingerbread cookies. As I unpacked, I looked around my room. The same pink curtains and pink bedspread with yellow pillows. The books on my shelves hadn't been moved. I cried and cried and cried and cried.

I got up around two a.m., and walked downstairs. I walked around the den and looked at the family pictures and my awards that still cluttered the bookcases in the den. I stared at my dad's brown leather recliner. I walked over to it and kicked it. How could he have let me go, how could he have not come to see me or tell me he loved me? I walked into the living room, then the dining room and made my way back to the kitchen. I took a glass out of the cabinet. It had faded brown and orange flowers on it.

Christmas came and went. I played cards with dad just as we used to. I realized my dad just wanted to sweep everything under the carpet and go on. He had gotten his way. His daughter was in college, getting the education he had never had, and that was all that was important.

New Year's Eve was cold and rainy, but Mom had insisted we drive into town for some groceries. Some families were coming over for games and movies. The kitchen cabinets were full of food, but I didn't protest. Instead of turning right on Highway 28, we turned left. Mom didn't say a word as we drove to the United Methodist Church. We parked and walked over to the graveyard. I walked slowly toward Carson's grave, the dead leaves and snow and ice crunching beneath my feet. My hands traced his name and the date. I kissed the top of the stone. It was cold and so quiet. I walked past the side of the church with the three stained glass windows. The church where I had grown up, gone to Vacation Bible Schools, had worked in the nursery, had sung in the choir. Where I had sat between Beck and Carson.

Back at home, folks started piling in. There were games in the den, a puzzle in the living room and the dining room table full of food. I laughed inside at how cozy it was here and how unlikely it was that I would ever fit in again. At 9:15, Chloe came in. I stayed in the living room, helping some of the younger children put the winter snow scene puzzle together.

And, as my counselor said, "Face it." First I went to the bathroom and as I was going out, there was Chloe. We stood face to face, and then she hugged me. I didn't know what to do. When the embrace ended, we both went back to the party.

The next day Chloe called and invited me over for lunch. I could hear Dad and Mom discussing it as I was getting dressed. It was the first time all break I had been on the front porch. I walked briskly by, not wanting to look, thinking that maybe Carson or Beck would mysteriously be sitting there. A dog barked. The old iron gate squeaked. I stayed the whole afternoon. We cried, we looked at pictures of Carson, talked about Beck.

Around four in the afternoon, I finally made my way back home. I stared at the front of my house. Mom had already turned on the Christmas lights, so it looked warm and welcoming. I stopped at the mailbox and stared. It was almost five when I opened the door and made my way into the house. The envelope of pictures was stuck in my coat and I quickly walked down the hall to my bedroom.

It would be a few more years before I would make it back home. Not much had changed. Yellow flowered glasses had replaced the brown and orange ones. Mr. Vanhorn moved the old Rambler from the side of the barn. The porch swing and old iron gate were the same.

Dad yelled at me to come into the den. My cousin was on the television as a newscaster. We sat there watching the news. It was cold and I wrapped the afghan around my legs. I was relieved when Mom called us in for dinner. I would be leaving in two days. Back to work, where the pace would be quicker and there would be no quiet home–cooked meals. I was ready to sort out life and love.

The next day I decided to take a long hike on the farm. So after a breakfast of homemade blueberry waffles I took my mom's collie, Rex, and headed out. I thought about Carson, Beck, and the daughter that I had, but would never know. I wondered what it would have been like if I would have stayed at home. What would have happened if Carson had not died? Would Beck have stayed around if he knew that I had carried his baby? Why didn't he come looking for me after his mom had told him? It was past two when I made my way back home. I was cold, tired and hungry, but there was something about the fresh air that renewed my hope and, for the first time, I forgave myself.

A large black car with New York plates was parked in Mr. Vanhorn's driveway. My heart began beating faster and I stop in my tracks.

It had to be Beck, who else? I wanted to figure out how I could get home without walking past their front living room window. The only way would to be backtrack around their barn and fence. It would be at least a mile. I forged ahead looking up at the sky. I heard the door open and the porch stairs creak. He lit a cigarette and walked the few steps to the sidewalk, then to the gate. I stood about ten feet away, at the mailbox. He cursed, as he had to push the snow away from the gate with his leather shoes to get it opened. He took another drag of his cigarette and tossed it into the snow. He was taller than I remembered. He pulled his wool, double–breasted coat closer to him.

"Hey, Leah I am sorry, so sorry." Beck said. I couldn't talk, I just stood there. Beck had tears in his eyes. I started to reach up and wipe them away. Instead, I grabbed his arm.

"I loved you, you know. I loved you more than I loved Carson."

Then I saw from the corner of my eye a woman staring out the big picture window. Beck stepped back from me, turned and waved to the girl.

"Leah, Leah." That is all he said as he turned and walked away. He didn't look back and I watched him walk up the steps as I made my way to my front gate.

I took a deep breath as I entered into the house. I excused myself to take a quick shower before dinner. In the shower, I cried. I pulled on my sweatpants and turtleneck, and slipped on a flannel shirt and thick socks. We ate dinner and then played a few board games. We discussed the next day, getting me to the airport, what time to leave.

The next morning, I was sitting in my bedroom, trying to sort out my last few years; thinking about how my life had taken a twist that I still was not sure how to handle. There was a knock at the door; I could hear Dad's voice. Beck was standing in my living room. For a split second, I remembered a fall night that Carson, Beck, and I had spent together. We had just finished watching something on television. Carson had gone to the bathroom and Beck walked up to me. I had something on the side of my face. He wiped it off and had then just stood still, staring at me.

We didn't sit on the front porch swing. Instead, we sat in his car on the cold leather seats. Knowing the pretty woman in the house would soon be sitting there made me squeamish. In the side pocket were some mints and eye cream. I wondered why the eye cream was in the car. I remembered I had seen the commercial, but at eighty–five dollars, an ounce I hadn't bought it. I twirled it nervously between my fingers.

Beck's presence was overwhelming. He was so handsome. Beck rubbed his hands together and then grabbed mine. I looked out at the glistening snow, the icicles melting along the side of the house. I started to cry. He pulled me close. I looked up, he muttered some curses, and hit his fist on the steering wheel. "Leah, I'm getting married. I am marrying the girl you saw in the window."

I hugged my mom and dad at the airport. As soon as I was seated, the air-line attendant walked up to me. She sat a nine–year–old girl next to me. She was traveling alone. We took turns reading the books from her backpack, working crossword puzzles and drawing. When the little girl asked if I was a mommy I didn't know how to answer.

I managed somehow to get off the plane. At the airport, I made my way to the first available chair. It was noisy with people shuffling back and forth. I watched as the mother and the little girl walked down the corridor hand in hand.

It would be years before I would see Beck again. I had moved back to the farm a year before. My dad had passed away and I decided to come be with my mom. Mr. Vanhorn had long been dead and Chloe had moved back to New York.

It was a fall day, but winter had decided to visit two days before, so there was snow and ice everywhere. The Vanhorn farm was up for sale.

I remember waking up that morning, the stillness so deep it required me to be quiet enough to hear.

We saw a car slowly make its way up Mr. Vanhorn's snowy driveway, then a second one. A few hours later only one car remained and then I watched as it slowly pulled out of the drive and into ours. Mom went to the door. Chloe ran up the steps and gave Mom a hug. I could see Beck sitting in the car. I noticed the wind was blowing so hard that the old front porch swing was moving rapidly back and forth, the chains creaking with each sway. The icicles on the porch were thick. Across the road on Mr. Vanhorn's old barn, a large icicle fell and crashed below onto the silent snow, as I watched Chloe and Beck drive down Winter's Lane.

What Did The Whippor Will?

*I*T WASN'T LOVE at first sight. Common sense prevailed, so Libby politely declined Addison's first request to have dinner. "Divorced with kids"—those words had helped her decline many invitations and opportunities. Although he was strong and handsome, kids and divorced rang in her ears. There were many words to describe Libby, but capricious wasn't one of them. She was an insurance rep for a large company when she met Addison McGary. Libby was busy and focused. She had never married and in the past five years hadn't dated much. Persistence on Addison's part convinced Libby to give him a chance; along with the fact that he seemed kind and considerate didn't hurt either.

Addison had two children and an ex–wife. Blaine, his son, and daughter Meryl. Libby wasn't concerned about meeting the ex–Mrs. McGary. They had not heard from her since Meryl's second birthday.

Addison lived up a long, narrow, gravel road, called Whipporwill Lane. As the story goes, Addison's great–grandfather, Bull McGary, often had to work two jobs. He usually found a ride to the end of town but had to walk the rest of the way home. He would be weary and the dark road was too quiet, but when he heard the whipporwills, he knew he only had a few miles to go.

Great Grandmother Izzy swore she always knew when Bull was almost home, usually around the time she was finishing the dishes. She said she would open the kitchen window because she could hear the whipporwills and she knew Bull was almost home. She would get her lantern and start walking down the road to meet him. They lived happily together for sixty years. They both died within six weeks of one another. Many years later when the county allowed residents to choose names of the roads on which they lived, Addison chose Whipporwill Lane.

This was the house that three generations of McGarys had lived in. The house was still adorned with Addison's boyhood, Boy Scout awards, ribbons from local and state fairs, and baseball pictures.

Libby fell in love with Addison, Blaine and Meryl all on the same day. It was their third date and her first time meeting the kids. She had driven out to Addison's home. It had an oversized porch that wrapped itself around the front of the old cozy farm house. They spent the day together. They rode horses, played in the stream, caught fish from the pond and fried them for dinner. They welcomed the night by eating watermelon and catching fireflies. They built a fire and sat around the porch, watching it from a distance. Libby looked over at Addison, watching him as he held Meryl in his arms and rocked her gently until she fell asleep.

In the brief time they dated, Libby grew not only to love him, but to respect him too. He was a no–nonsense type of businessman, but at the same time a gentle and patient father. He played football with Blaine, but also brushed Meryl's long blonde hair every night. Meryl could brush her own hair but she loved for her daddy to, so it was a nightly ritual. Libby would watch as they played long games of cards. She was still amazed at how he had kept up his rigorous schedule he'd had since he became a single dad. He got up early every morning and worked on the farm. He came back in at seven, got the kids up, made them breakfast and after they caught the bus, he was back in the fields. Their nightly dinner was a group effort and after dinner and home-work, they all went to bed.

After six months of dating, Addison decided to ask Libby to spend the rest of her life with him. One night after the kids had gone to bed and the sun had set, Addison proposed to Libby. He was sitting on the swing; she was sitting on the porch steps. He said it was time for Libby to watch the sunrise on the farm, not just the sunsets. "Will you please think about being my wife and a mother to my children? The kids and I love you."

They both stood up at the same time and started walking toward each other. Libby, who never got nervous, was so jittery she tripped over her glass of lemonade. Addison tried to catch her but when he stuck out his arm, instead of catching her, he accidentally pushed Libby and she fell off the porch and into a large bush. They both were laughing as Libby managed her way out of the bush, landing in Addison's strong arms. They kissed and, through tears, Libby said "yes."

They married on a cool September evening in the backyard of the farmhouse on Whipporwill Lane.

They honeymooned in a quaint bed and breakfast in Bar Harbor, Maine. They took morning bike rides and long afternoon naps. They were gone two full weeks, the longest Addison had ever been away from his children. He missed them terribly and Libby surprised herself by how much she thought of them.

On their first night back from the honeymoon, Addison insisted on preparing Libby's first bath in their house. So after the kids were asleep, Libby obliged. She could hear Addison humming as he drew the water.

Addison claimed as much as Libby loved the porch, she would love the bathtub more. The old farmhouse had a large clawfoot tub. Above the left side of the tub was a huge window. Above the sink, the window was so old it had to be propped open with a stick. He said his mama used to run the raccoons away from the back porch with the same stick.

He kissed Libby on the forehead, and then dimmed the light as he left the bathroom. She lowered herself into the warm bubbly water as the cool September breeze seeped through the window. She could hear him whistling in the kitchen. She smiled contentedly.

She had a full view of the moon and stars. She could see the old elm tree swaying and hear the weeping willow swishing against the ground. Libby adjusted the towel behind her head. Addison had promised her a "Twinkle and Glitter" show. It was breathtaking and Libby was at peace. The smell of the night air seemed to penetrate into the depths of her soul, refreshing her. She could hear the crickets, owls, and a coyote or two but, above all, the whipporwills. Their sound was like a lullaby and Libby was more content than she had ever been in her life.

Libby's first bath lasted close to two hours. It ended only when Addison came in, scooped her out of the tub, wrapped her into a quilt and carried her through the house, dripping water. She laughed and held tight as Addison took her to the swing on the back porch. "Beautiful," she whispered, watching the fireflies light up the night sky. Addison dried the ends of her hair with the quilt. She snuggled deeper into the quilt and fell asleep in Addison arms to the sound of the creaking porch swing. She didn't hear him when he promised her a life of long love just like the love Bull and Izzy had shared.

The next few months were a whirlwind as Libby adjusted easily to being a wife and struggled at being a mother. She had lived an independent life before this and although she loved the kids, she looked forward to the sound of the bus in the morning, knowing the next eight hours didn't require her to be a mother. Libby also remembers though, the first time she looked at the clock, waiting for the kids to come home from school, anticipating hearing about their day.

Libby was content and happy. She loved the farm; she loved walking out in the fields in the middle of the day or to the barn and watching Addison work. She learned about fields, crops, planting, fixing tractors, horses. She loved the secure feeling she had when she could see her life here.

One dreary November day, Blaine found Libby curled up in the overstuffed, worn brown chair, staring out the window. He was expecting to follow their usual routine of having a snack and then going to find his dad out in the fields, but it was not to be.

Just yesterday, Addison had sat in that brown chair. He had insisted Libby come sit on his lap and look at a new farm magazine. He became so excited as he showed her his plans for the farm that Libby laughed. Although he should have been working, they had spent the afternoon, talking, laughing, in that big brown chair. They had barely gotten their clothes back on when the kids came home from school.

Now, how could she tell them? She was about to turn their world upside down. Addison had been killed at nine–thirty that morning in a tractor accident. The morning started out as usual, but Libby decided to surprise Addison with a picnic lunch. As she crossed over the first field, she could hear his tractor running as if it were stuck. She saw the tractor, but not Addison. She started to panic; the closer she got, the louder the tractor, and still no sign of Addison. Then she found him lying on the ground, covered with mud and blood. She screamed repeatedly and lay down beside his lifeless body, clinging to him. She kissed his cheek and his lips. She grabbed his hand and then dropped it. She sat beside him, her head rested on her knees, rocking. She stood up, smelling the blood in her long hair.

The ambulance, the police, the neighbors. They came, they went.

Afterwards, Libby gathered the kids into her arms and they sank awkwardly into the chair, each staring out the window. She was not sure when the kids left her lap or what the kids did for the next few hours. When a knock on the door startled her, she realized that she was now the one in charge. The kids probably needed her and their dinner. Libby appreciatively accepted a warm glass dish from Mrs. Davis and barely remembered closing the door.

She walked into the kitchen. The kids were just sitting there. Meryl had a blue crayon and was drawing a tractor on a piece of yellow construction paper. Blaine had his pocket knife out, trying to sharpen a stick. She set the dish down and gathered Blaine and Meryl in her arms. They sank to the floor and cried. When she realized it was after eight, she kissed their foreheads and suggested they should all try to eat. She stood there as their trembling lips tried to eat and big tears fell down their cheeks, spilling onto their food. In a little over one year, she had become a wife, mother, and now a widow.

Libby found it difficult being a single mother; she was barely surviving being a widow, so she tried desperately to find Blaine and Meryl's mother. Maybe their mother had matured. Perhaps now she missed them and wanted to be in their lives. She called everyone and anyone who might have known where Addison's ex–wife was, but to no avail. Addison's ex did not want to be found.

At night when she tucked in Blaine and Meryl, two pairs of big brown eyes would ask what words couldn't, "Are you leaving too?" She would tuck them in tightly, read to them and swear everything would be okay. Almost nightly she would go to the porch, and sit in the rocker or on the steps, but not in the porch swing. She would cry and wonder how she was going to make it. She would be exhausted but would wander aimlessly through the house, then to the porch and then back to the house, and end up sleeping in the brown worn chair.

Many days after she got the kids off to school, she would go sit in the barn, lie on the hay and remember her and Addison's short time together.

As time went on, Libby made some tough decisions. Libby dug in her heels and learned about farming, more than she ever thought she would need to know. She kept the farm, but downsized the livestock and horses, and leased some of the fields. Money was tight, but every month she managed to pay the bills. And most important, she and the children learned to live without Addison.

One night she went to check on Blaine and Meryl. Two of Addison's farm magazines lay under Blaine's pillow. Meryl lay under her purple and pink comforter with one of Addison's unsightly old work boots tucked under her small arm. Libby crawled in beside her, but couldn't sleep. And so went their days.

One cold December night, a week before school break, Libby was miserable and she knew the kids were too. It was going to be their second Christmas without their father. It seemed it was going to be tough. Last year they were in shock and the reality had not set in. Their pain and grief had not subsided.

The children sat in the kitchen trying to do their homework. They couldn't concentrate and when Libby raised her voice enough to bring Meryl to tears, she knew they needed a break. Libby was at loss as to what to do. What she wanted was to pack her bags and go back to her safe life, one that didn't afford time to think about all the lonely, empty places in her heart. She felt deserted and, even worse, deserted with two children to care for.

Eventually they ended up in Addison's closet. They all just sat in the small closet, sharing memories, laughing. Blaine took a wool cap and put it on. Libby followed by donning a flannel shirt, and Meryl, a pair of muddy work boots. They were all laughing as the boots weighed as much as Meryl.

They decided to go outside and build a fire and roast marshmallows. After they had sat around awhile, Blaine took Addison's hat off and threw it into the fire. Libby and Meryl were shocked, but then Meryl threw one of his boots in, then the other. It seemed they thought of the same thing simultaneously. At once they ran back into the house and grabbed tractor and farming magazines. They ran back outside and threw the magazines into the fire.

It was well past midnight when they came inside. They needed baths but Libby was too tired to fight about it. Instead, they crawled into bed with Libby. Libby wasn't sure it was best to let them skip school the next day, but she did. They wanted brownies and ice cream for breakfast, and she acceded. They sat around the wooden table, smelling of smoke, eating huge spoonfuls of ice cream and warm chewy brownies. Libby couldn't imagine loving any two kids more nor could she imagine how she was going to raise them, but she knew without a doubt she would.

The years passed quickly, and Libby soon found herself with two teenagers. Blaine, like Addison, had a love for the farm. Any minute he wasn't in school, Blaine could be found working on the farm. Blaine was steady and level-headed. He was handsome and caring, and he and Libby got along fine. Meryl, on the other hand, was independent and restless and wanted to be away from the farm as much as possible. A far too familiar sight was Blaine coming home from the fields to find Meryl and Libby arguing. Meryl was fifteen, dressing as if she were twenty and acting as if she were two. Blaine was able to reconcile them at times, and the fighting would cease for a few days.

Blaine came home again to find Libby curled up in the brown overstuff leather chair. She had the same look on her face the day they had lost Addison. Although the chair had been reupholstered, it was now worn again. Over the years the kids refused to sit in it, but Libby refused to let it go. She repeated to Blaine the words Meryl had spoken a few hours earlier, "Meryl is pregnant! Did you hear me, Blaine? Meryl is pregnant."

As the months passed, discussions took place and decisions were made. Meryl would have the baby and stay at the farm for the first six weeks. Then she would move into an apartment in town, close to the high school. The school had a program for unwed mothers, so Meryl could complete her sophomore year. She would spend the weekends on the farm. Meryl refused to tell anyone who the father was. Libby was having doubts that Meryl even knew who it was.

Libby awoke early the day Meryl and Walker were to move out. It was such a joy, more than Libby realized, having Walker around. He was a beautiful baby and she was amazed at how he had so quickly stolen her heart. He had a big round head and blue eyes. Libby was going to miss not having him near her every day.

She had lost track of time and realized it was almost seven and Meryl wasn't up. Blaine's friends were going to be showing up anytime to help them with the move. She went up to Meryl's room and tapped on the door. There was no answer, so she gently pushed the door open. The unmade bed held a note. Walker lay sleeping in the bassinet. Libby screamed when she read the note, startling Walker, who began to cry. She grabbed him and ran outside to find Blaine. She slipped in the mud and fell down with Walker in her arms. She sat in the mud, feeling it slowly seep through her jeans and the tail of her shirt.

The days passed into weeks and Meryl's silent absence loomed large in their hearts. Libby and Blaine interviewed Meryl's former friends and followed every lead. No one seemed to know where Meryl went or with whom she went.

"Blow out your candles Walker, you can do it, blow hard." Walker's blue eyes grew big as he tried with all his might to blow out the three small candles. Libby was trying to balance Walker on the picnic bench as he tried.

Not only was it Walker's birthday party, but also Blaine's going–away party. Blaine was going to college. Blaine had begged Libby to let him stay at home one more year and help her on the farm. She had insisted that the sooner he went, the sooner he would be back. Libby wanted him to get an education. He had been such a tower of strength to Libby, but he needed to go, to discover life outside of his surroundings.

The plan was for him to get a degree in agriculture and then come back to run the farm. Blaine wanted to implement the vision Addison had for the farm and land so many years ago. For the time being, he would come back on the weekends. Libby knew she needed to hire someone to help her and had promised Blaine she would run an ad in the local paper soon.

Walker, with icing all over his lips, walked over to Libby and climbed into her lap. He was tired. His full day of fun, without a nap, was catching up with him. She kissed his head as he sat contentedly. They watched the rest of the gang as they danced and played ball.

She caught a glance of Blaine out of the corner of her eye. He was leaning against a tree, catching fireflies for the little children. He caught her eye and winked and mouthed, "You are a great mom." Libby did not allow the ensuing tear to fall from her eye and instead caught it with her finger.

Walker was a joy. Although it was hard running a farm and raising a baby, somehow she managed. Walker, as young as he was, had a spirit of wisdom, Libby discovered when she did farm business. As she took him into town to do business, or if someone came to the farm, she would observe Walker. If he would readily go toward someone, then it seemed their business deals were successful and honest. If Walker didn't smile or walk towards someone, she learned to be leery of doing business with them as she had gotten burned a few times. Walker seemed to know whom to trust and whom not to trust.

Libby remembered once in particular when someone wanted her to accept a personal check for a horse she was selling. It was her policy to accept only cashier's checks but she acceded. All during the business transaction, Walker had clung to Libby's leg. The check had bounced and she had lost a horse.

Libby slid quietly down into the tub. She could hear Blaine putting Walker down for the night. It was their ritual and Libby appreciated the help. She was ready for some alone time by the end of the day and Walker adored Blaine. Libby wondered how they would survive without Blaine. He would be home most weekends but she was so determined for him to get good grades, she wasn't sure if coming home so much would be in his best interest.

The first three weeks Blaine was gone, Libby didn't get much work done. Walker sensed the change and, missing Blaine, clung to her. The nights seemed so long. Although she was tired and Walker was asleep, she couldn't. She would take her tea and sit outside on the porch, listening to the whipporwills. She cried a lot. She thought about Addison and how much he would have loved Walker. She thought of Meryl and wondered where she was and why she had not called or shown any concern for her son.

On a cold October day, Libby was pulling her orange wool sweater over her head when it got stuck in her ponytail. Walker was playing on the porch when she heard someone talking to him. She briskly went to the door. There sat Walker in his coveralls and rubber boots, his nose red and smiling up at the stranger on the porch. Perhaps someone was responding to the ad she had run in the local paper.

"How can I help you?" Libby asked.

"Will Crawford is my name," the stranger said as they shook hands. Then he blurted out, "I think that Jake, my son . . . . well, he knew your daughter Meryl."

Libby grabbed the unstable porch swing. She wobbled a little while trying to gain her composure. She invited him in. Will helped Walker carry in a few of his toy tractors. Libby went to get some coffee. When she returned, she almost spilled the tray. Will was on the floor playing with Walker and his tractors. Walker was sitting on Will's lap. For the first time, Libby noticed that Walker looked exactly like Will.

Long after Walker was asleep, Will confirmed what was evident by the resemblance. Jake was Walker's father. Jake had met Meryl at a rodeo and, well, they all knew the rest. Jake had been killed just a few months earlier in an automobile accident, coming home from a football game. Will had finally gone through Jake's room, found some letters, and put two and two together. Libby's head was spinning.

As the months passed, Will spent more and more time at the farm, getting to know his grandson and helping with the work around the farm. Every day Libby, Will and Walker ate lunch together. One day as Libby was washing the dishes, Will grabbed her wet, soapy hand. He dried it off and they stood in the kitchen. He kissed her and Libby once again fell in love on Whipporwill Lane.

"Walker, hurry up", Blaine impatiently waited for Walker at the top of the stairs, but with a big grin and outstretched arms. "Come on, buddy, it is time." Blaine said.

Walker and Blaine stood on either side of Libby and escorted her down the grass aisle. Libby and Will were married in the spring, on a Sunday afternoon, surrounded by a small group of friends. They danced and celebrated well into the night.

Libby and Will stayed on the farm, along with Walker and Blaine. Meryl contacted them only once, asking for money. She did not ask about Walker.

The Thin Line Of The Crow's Feet

SHELBY REALIZED how tired she was as she got into her car. There would be no turning back now as she had dropped off a few boxes at the second–hand store. She laid her head on the car headrest and sat there for a few moments. No pretending how exciting the journey would be, this was the real thing. Everything she owned was now neatly stacked in one of the bedrooms on Aunt Ellie's second floor. Her feet were on the path, her fears mingled with the excitement. It wasn't as if there was much to keep her at home but something had kept her there the last fifteen years. Shelby shed a few tears. Only two more days to say her goodbyes. She realized the coming loneliness of not getting to see Aunt Ellie on a daily basis. Her plan of being gone for two years did not sound so "right" now. Could she do this? Could she walk out this dream? It was right before her and all she wanted to do was to crawl in bed with her favorite quilt and hide.

She had submitted her proposal for three years and got back nothing but rejection letters. She had contacted universities, hospitals, senior citizen magazines and many other organizations to help finance this undertaking.

She could still recall the day the letter arrived from a small university back east. They were interested in meeting with her to discuss the proposed project. Within two weeks, she was sitting in a room with university department heads and a few deans. Most of them caught the vision quickly. She dealt successfully with the few cynics that were present in the room. She proposed to travel across the country interviewing couples who had been married for thirty years or longer, questioning them about their health, the reasons their marriage worked, their income levels, children, education, and a thousand other questions. After the interviews were over, she would compile all her notes and conclusions into a book. Their grant money would cover seventy–five percent of the project. Now it was time. Time to walk out the dream. Could she really stay away for two years? Would this project be as successful as she dreamed it would be?

Shelby snapped herself back into focus and savored the short walk to the back door. How she loved this house! A brick home laid out on two flat beautiful acres. Flower gardens placed strategically throughout the back yard. The second floor with its two bedrooms joined by a sitting area was where she had stored the few things she couldn't part with. The rooms hadn't been used for years.

Bitterness interrupted her thoughts. Shane, the owner of the newspaper she had worked for, had guaranteed partial financing for this project. She had known Shane since seventh grade. Yes, she had, through the years turned down his marriage proposals, but he should have been over her by now. Wasn't he married? Wasn't he the owner of the newspaper? She realized the mistake of dating him in high school. Like all those young decisions, should they be carved in concrete?

It all seemed so romantic then, her becoming a writer and photographer, their plans to work together. "Oh, brother," Shelby sighed. She had enjoyed her time at the local newspaper, despite Shane. She was the staff writer along with doing freelance photography on the side.

She had tried to leave one other time. She dreamed of working for a major photography magazine. They accepted a few of her pieces but never offered her consistent work, although she had assured them she would have no trouble traveling all over the world. They communicated quite clearly that they preferred males because it was less complicated than hiring females who might subordinate their needs to those of a husband and children. In addition, it wasn't safe for females to travel where they would need her to go.

She couldn't believe her bungalow had sold so quickly. She had loved the house she grew up in with Aunt Ellie, but Aunt Ellie had insisted Shelby buy her own home because she thought Shelby needed her space. She had bought this bungalow just four blocks away from her Aunt Ellie.

Her friends were elated she was finally "leaving town" as they often referred to the change in her career. They could not offer her any sympathy on the woes involved in leaving her aunt. Her three best friends were scattered about California, Massachusetts, and Washington. Throughout the years, they had all begged her to move to the cities where they lived.

"I have arrived," she said aloud. However, upon "arrival," the world didn't look safe. Was this project too much of a risk? What if the couples didn't like her? What if they didn't talk? What if after all the interviews, she found nothing of relevance? What if no one wanted to buy her book? What if she didn't live up to the university's expectations? Random thoughts and questions jumbled Shelby's usually level head. Instead of feeling secure in a ship in which she was sailing away, she felt as if she were in a johnboat tossing about in a white squall.

Etched clearly in her mind was the day she had named the project, many, many years before its inception. In the midst of death, the dream was born. She was at her parents' funeral, sitting next to her grandmother. Shelby noticed how wrinkled her grandmother's hands looked and how she smelled like hairspray. She watched a tear fall from her grandmother's eye and thread itself gently through the lines. She had not noticed until then how many lines were around her grandmother's eyes. Shelby later learned they were begrudgingly called "crow's feet." Then she scanned the room where a rather large crowd had gathered. What made some live longer than others? How many were content with their lives? She looked around at the few who were still married and wondered how they had made it. She wondered about her parents' marriage for the first time in her life. Had her parents been happy? Had they had a good marriage? What is a good marriage? She would never know and it made her angry thinking of how little she knew about her parents and, up until then, had never cared.

She was fifteen at the time. She couldn't cry at her parents' funeral but the next year when her grandmother died, the reservoir was released. She had closed her heart to any feeling, and if it hadn't been for Aunt Ellie, she wouldn't have survived.

She looked down at the satchel she carried. It contained the names and places she would soon put faces to. The list emanated hope. She would trek across America to the homes of people she didn't know, to interview, to delve into their hearts and lives. She loved the green Suburban in which she sat, a last minute surprise, loaned to her by the local car dealership. The new leather smelled wonderful and she felt giddy, as if she had never before sat behind a wheel. She had laid out her route and map many times before today. She and Aunt Ellie had gone over it step by step so that every day Aunt Ellie would know where Shelby was going and where she had been.

After a restless night and an early breakfast, Shelby said goodbye to the world surrounding her. Looking out the rearview mirror, she watched as Aunt Ellie stood on the porch waving, then noticing a weed, stooped down to pull it from the flowers that decorated the corner of the porch.

Her first stop was six hours away. When she arrived in the new city, fear ripped through her. Questions began to bombard her. What had she gotten herself into? Would she be able to sleep in all the different homes? What if this project was too intrusive and no one wanted to open their personal lives to a complete stranger? What if she failed? What would it feel like to fail?

Her first stop was at the home of John and Cora Madden. They were warm and welcoming. When the first night came to an end, she laid her head down on the cold, crisp sheets and felt her body take to the well worn–mattress. The bath had refreshed her, as did the home–cooked meal. She had sworn off fried foods years ago, but she knew there would be concessions to make. The chicken was good, and the apple pie made her feel warm and secure. Cora and John were kind and a little lonely, Shelby sensed. There was a sadness in their eyes and Shelby hoped she would find out why.

The next morning Shelby was awakened by a tractor. It wasn't even seven. Unbeknownst to Shelby, John had been up two hours and had put off mowing so she could sleep in. Cora had fresh fruit and muffins on a tattered tablecloth, but it was the black coffee on the counter that Shelby wanted.

Shelby spent the morning with Cora and the plan was to spend time with John in the afternoon. Shelby took out the tape player, and started asking questions. The precious couple had been married forty–four years. Shelby helped Cora make apple pies for a church dinner. Shelby cut apples until her fingers ached but she had a wonderful time. Cora was a no-nonsense, but gentle, warm woman. Her long gray hair was brushed back into a ponytail holder, braided and wrapped down the middle of her back.

Cora had met John at a church picnic. Shelby's thoughts raced ahead as if to plan the story. They had fallen in love, of course, in a meeting of the eye. As the other boys choose to go down to the creek and skip rocks, John had gone off and picked Cora a bouquet of wild-flowers. Four months later, they were engaged. As the romance blossomed, her parents had great objections, money being the main one.

The two eloped after a high school dance, driving to a small Arkansas town. It was rumored that Cora was pregnant, but anyone who knew John would know that he was a gentleman then as much as he is now. The rumor was simply not true.

Cora and John arrived back at her parents' house to announce their marriage. The atmosphere was tense. Cora's eyes filled with tears as she continued to relate the story to Shelby. "I learned my father had an affair with John's mom after I was born. They all knew each other since the town was small. My mom had been ill after I was born and she suffered from depression for six months. John's mom was a beautiful lady and, well, it just happened once. After the big announcement, we went to John's parents. They were fond of me. John's dad never knew about the affair. I love John's mom now as much as I did then. She knew I knew when I told her about how my parents had reacted. Years passed, the kids came and life just went on. The sad thing is my mom never hugged me as she did before I was married. Visits from my parents became more and more infrequent. My dad committed suicide two weeks after my second son was born. Mom followed the next month."

Shelby felt overwhelmed by Cora's grief. A quick look at the clock ensured that it would soon be time to join John in the field. Relief swept over Shelby. Cora began to make lunch.

John wiped his feet at the door and carefully rinsed the dirt off his worn fingers. He then kissed his wife on the cheek. Cora finished his lunch and poured his drink. Shelby sensed much respect and honor between them and wondered if she would find that with all of the couples?

It was good to be outside. John graciously took more breaks than usual so Shelby could keep up with him. He talked of life on the farm, crops, and the price of an acre of land. He also spoke of Cora's pain. Although he thought this project was interesting, he was more comfortable with the more general questions.

Shelby hugged them both, far too long, before she left. As John closed the driver's side door, Cora laid a handmade quilt on the passenger seat, saying they were waiting to give it to someone special. Shelby promised she would keep in touch. How would she handle it, if she felt this attached to every couple? She wanted to stay with them, drink lemonade and smell the freshly mown grass.

She wanted to somehow bottle the serenity she felt at their home.

She had driven the day with the quilt on her lap. Shelby was elated, all light and joyful inside, as she wrote. She had made better time than she'd thought she would and arrived at the hotel a few hours ahead of schedule.

The days turned into weeks. Shelby was either driving, interviewing, or sitting in a hotel room, typing up all the notes she had taken.

Most days she managed to call Aunt Ellie but on the days she couldn't, a twinge of homesickness would set in.

Shelby was tired when she arrived at the next family. From the moment Shelby met the couple, they kept her on her toes as they snapped at one another. Shelby pulled out her paper and pen and began asking questions.

"I don't know, I guess I am just stupid!" declared the woman. "I put up with him this long, what's another twenty?"

"Ha, woman, no one else would put up with you! You better be glad you got me." And so it would go, teasing and sarcasm mixed in their conversations. The day with them was unsettling. They didn't talk to each other, more at each other. Their expensive home had been paid for by his position of being a banker. They had no children. To fill the years they traveled frequently. They didn't have the warmth or joy of the last couple. They didn't pat each other or offer each other a drink although they had plenty of time now to serve one another. He went to the post office, returning two hours later. She left Shelby to go play bridge. It had been made clear Shelby wasn't invited to join her.

Shelby walked around their home and admired the art. When they both returned, they took her out for a nice meal. Shelby was tired and wanted the evening to be done after they returned from dinner, but they insisted she come down to the parlor. This very classy couple looked out of place there. She was rubbing his feet. It seemed out of character for the staunch couple. He then slowly poured lotion over her old hands and gently rubbed each finger. Shelby, for the first time that day, relaxed. She sipped on a glass of wine.

He began talking about how he had met her. She had gone to a bar, her first and last time. "I didn't like it then and I don't want to go to them now," she declared. He pursued her. She had never been pursued and decided to take the opportunity as it might be the only one. Did she love him? Shelby wondered. Four months later, they were engaged. Her wealthy parents were relieved that someone who didn't need their money was marrying her. They spoke more excitedly of the paintings in the room and their travels than the questions she was asking. She patted him softly and said, "I am tired," and for the first time, he smiled at her.

As Shelby walked down the long hallway to her room, she was suddenly aware of how lonely she was. She wanted someone to rub her back, to take their strong hands and caress them over her body. Shelby sighed as she stared into the bathroom mirror. She slept well in the queen–size bed that adorned the well–decorated room.

She arrived at the hotel around four the next day. She needed to type up some notes and check her E–mail. She had wanted Aunt Ellie to get a computer, but Aunt Ellie declined. "Call me," she would insist. Aunt Ellie wanted to make sure there was no homesickness in Shelby's voice. Shelby was trying to sound cheerful and upbeat. She hung up the phone and woke up at six. She hadn't intended to nap. She needed to work.

She started typing, took a break, did some sit ups, and then returned to her typing.

She wished she had never stopped at the Ralstins'. In this sleepy town where they tried to make a living, he went on the road as a truck driver, she working at local factories that would set up shop for a time.

Shelby arrived after seven, and that is when Mrs. Ralstin began talking. At nine–thirty, it seemed she finally took a breath. Mr. Ralstin sat in front of the television for the evening. He seldom spoke but when he did, he was crude and demanding.

"Woman, you better shut up in there, or I'll have to teach you another lesson." His harsh, demeaning words didn't seem to faze the woman.

After a fitful night of sleep, Shelby woke to the smell of coffee. Mrs. Ralstin started talking before Shelby's first sip.

"Why married so long? I didn't have anywhere else to go." She hung her head for a moment, but then went back to rambling. She had gotten her first "lesson" three days after they were married. She had fixed breakfast the first day. The second, she just hadn't thought of it. He didn't talk to her for the rest of the day. The third day of their marriage, she woke up to the physical pain that would continue throughout her marriage. He dragged her to the kitchen and explained that he would have breakfast every morning. "Don't make me remind you again!" he bellowed as he left for work. Shelby sat there, stunned. Mrs. Ralstin was so matter–of–fact.

Shelby laid her hand on her stomach. She felt nauseated. She laid her head back on the flat hotel pillow and cried. She then deleted a few paragraphs. She just couldn't write about all the pain and abuse, which unfortunately was still taking place. Shelby had sneaked out the door just a few hours earlier.

As Shelby moved on to her next stop, Bud Clarkson greeted Shelby in overalls and apologized for the grease on his hands. Blythe

Clarkson's warm greeting was a hug which made Shelby instantly feel at home.

Homemade bread and beans were served for lunch. Their home was modest with no air–conditioning and decorations hung awkwardly on the walls, but precious memories and love seemed to seep out of every room.

"I am going back to work," Bud said. Blythe put her hands on her hips and begged him not to go. "Now, honey, you know I have to go and it is not a big deal. They need my help." He pecked her on the cheek and lightly tapped her bottom. She laughed and dried her hands on her apron. Shelby hadn't noticed the apron before and realized she couldn't remember seeing anyone in an apron before.

"He is going back out to the shop. The doctor told him weeks ago to slow down. Then two weeks ago, his best friend died of a heart attack. Blythe collected herself within a few uncomfortable silent moments, which spoke volumes. She pulled out a pan and started preparing for dinner. They snapped beans and peeled potatoes. Blythe apologized for her meager home. It was comfortable and clean, and Shelby felt very at home.

Blythe began her story. She had come from a wealthy home with no love. She met Bud when she was eighteen and on her way to college. He was a grocery store clerk. She remembered their first soda together on the back steps of that store. When she announced to her parents she would not be going to college but marrying Bud Clarkson, they laughed. Then, they begged. Then gave an ultimatum. She realized she had to make a choice. She was about to give up a lot. She wanted her luxuries, the nice home, the pretty dresses. If she chose those things, there would be no Bud.

He didn't make any promises and told her to count the cost. He loved her, but that is all he had. Would it be enough? It has been hard and there were regrets. Her dad never did break, never did share his wealth, even when he was old and saw their meager home, humbly decorated.

She had left Bud once. "Growing up, I got a new dress every month. In many of my married years, I never got a new dress." Bud wasn't sympathetic but was always kind. "I went home for two weeks. Momma bought me clothes and had my hair done and offered me my old life back. However, after two weeks, I missed him. He did not come calling; I knew he would not. I would have to come home on my own. He would be there. I returned with all my new belongings and lined them up in my closet with the old worn dresses. They would have cost Bud two years' worth of wages. I never wore them. Every time I put them on, I felt distracted, detached—a different person. But I never gave them away. I can still remember Bud's face on my return. He cried."

After leaving the Clarkson's time seem to pass by even quicker. Shelby was ecstatic. Everything seemed to be falling in place. She was halfway through her travels. Could over a year have really gone by? She had interviewed so many people, stayed in so many homes, poor to wealthy and everything in–between. She felt the project was going better than she ever imagined. It was all wonderful, but the new places and people were beginning to wear on her. She had two more stops and then she was going to have a short respite. She was grateful for the pre–planned vacation.

She was tired and she wanted to be home with Aunt Ellie. She cried as she read her E–mails and caught up on paperwork. She could hardly believe she had been on this project as long as she had. She had many stories and tons of research material but working all the time in hotels and other people's homes was taking its toll. Only two more stops, and then she was would stay at a bed and breakfast called the Shelby Inn. The name, of course, is partly why she chose it.

Ingram and Lillie McCann were grandparents raising their twin grandchildren. Their only child, Marie, married a wonderful man, Lane, and had twins. Marie and Lane went on a vacation, their first without their four–year–old twins. The plane went down and, at fifty–five, Ingram and Lillie had become parents instead of grandparents. They loved the girls, but it wasn't easy. Their passports, like their dreams, lay dormant upstairs, tucked away in a dresser drawer.

The next stop, her last before her vacation, was only two hours away. So in no time at all, Shelby pulled off onto the gravel driveway, just as the directions had said. A tire lay on its side with poppies blooming in it. Turning a curve, she saw a lady walking in the middle of the drive. She waved and Shelby rolled down her window, and they introduced themselves. The lady was Mildred Bradford, the wife in the next couple she was to visit.

Mildred teared up. "They buried my husband two days ago," she said.

"Oh, my." Shelby's heart instantly ached. Shelby turned off the ignition and they sat on the road. Shelby offered to leave, since she did not want to intrude, but Mildred insisted she stay. After about an hour, as the sun was disappearing, they finished the mile drive up to the house. As Shelby was helping Mildred up the porch steps, the screen door burst open. It startled Shelby. She had assumed no one was there.

Their eyes met, and she gulped as Mildred introduced Gabe, her son. They shook hands. She noticed the side of his jaw and the small scar on his neck. He smiled and said he really had been looking forward to meeting her ever since his mom had written about the project.

She felt uncomfortable and again offered to leave. She felt like an intruder. Shelby looked around the room. Traces of activity were everywhere: casserole dishes, cards scattered on the coffee table, flowers, half–empty coffee cups. Mildred and Gabe assured her she was welcome and talked about Holt's death. They said they needed a break from all the sadness and shock of the past week. Holt had been feeling bad, but, as usual, resisted going to the doctor. Mildred had gone to the barn when he hadn't come in for lunch. She had found him slumped over a bale of hay.

The next day Mildred left before Shelby woke up. She left a note for Shelby. Mildred had to take care of some financial things in town and asked Shelby to please spend some time with Gabe. She assured Shelby that Gabe could answer the questions that were intended for Holt.

Gabe entered the back door of the kitchen as she was just finishing the note. He had a wonderful big smile. A little too confident, thought Shelby. As soon as Shelby finished her cup of tea, they headed outside. He started in with questions, seemingly genuinely interested in her project. They walked down the gravel road towards the river. They spent the day walking around the farm. It was a large farm with barns, animals, ponds, and gardens. The day passed quickly.

Mildred looked tired and it was easy to see the day had been hard on her. They ate a light dinner and Mildred promised to give Shelby her side of the story and correct Gabe's stories of the day. She smiled and patted Shelby's shoulder. Mildred lightly kissed Gabe's cheek and for a moment, time stood still, the breeze was blowing and somewhere in the woods a small animal scurried about in the leaves. Such a love between this family! Shelby suddenly felt sad that she had never met Holt.

It would be a lie to say she wasn't a little excited to spend more time with Gabe. The day with him had been wonderful although she'd learned a long time ago not to go imagining or dreaming or hoping in regards to romance. Gabe brought out a couple cups of hot chocolate and they watched the fireflies from the back steps. Way after midnight, they finally went into the house. She still had not gone down the hallway, which had a bedroom on each side, Gabe's on one side and Mildred's on the other.

She wondered what it would have been like to fall asleep next to someone for forty-six years and, in one day, have it all change.

Gabe hadn't really talked about himself, just that he had been traveling. So when Mildred woke up fresh and ready to talk, Gabe left to do some things around the farm. Shelby learned a lot. Mildred answered her questions, intermingling Gabe's life story with her own. Gabe had spent the last twelve years in India and Africa as a freelance photographer, but mostly made his living from assignments from a major magazine. Mildred led Shelby down the hallway to his room, which was covered with pictures he had taken and places he had been.

She was wondering when he would return and if she had remembered to ask Mildred all the questions she should. She listened for the sound of his boots on the porch and felt guilty for thinking of him.

Mildred retired early and Shelby needed to get some notes down but instead had dozed in the old rocker until Gabe startled her by touching her shoulder. It was after nine. He didn't talk, just stood in front of her and held out his hand.

They didn't say a word as he led her by the hand out the door, across the porch, past the barn, and down the grassy hill. They walked around the pond; the frogs were croaking, and the moon danced its way across the murky pond water. He took her by the shoulders, lifted up her head and kissed her. He held her tight; then they made their way slowly back to the barn. They sat inside the barn on a pile of hay looking out watching the stars, Shelby's head resting gently on Gabe's broad shoulder.

Mildred gently tapped on the bedroom door. Shelby had slept later than she intended. Mildred handed her a cup of tea and sat on the edge of the bed. "When is your next stop scheduled? I know you are supposed to leave today." Shelby was supposed to check into Shelby Inn by seven that night.

Mildred took her hand, "I know you need a break but you are welcome to stay here. I am a mom and I won't intrude. Well, I won't intrude too much," she winked at Shelby. "Gabe will be here until Thursday. Couldn't you stay until then?" Shelby easily accepted the request.

"What did Gabe want?" she wondered. He greeted her warmly and told her to dress comfortably because they were going for a drive and a hike. Shelby begged Mildred to go with them, but Mildred had wanted to go through some of Holt's things, alone.

Gabe talked about all his adventures in India and Africa. They drove for a little over an hour and, in fact, Shelby was a little nauseated. She was tired, excited, and confused, and realized she hadn't eaten enough over the last few days. Gabe took her to the house and land that he had grown-up on. They still owned the property, but no one had lived there since they had moved Gabe's senior year. It was beautiful. It was Gabe's place and after his travels, his plan was to move back there.

After lunch they hiked up a small trail. Gabe laid a blanket on the ground where they would have a perfect view of the overlook. The panoramic view was breathtaking. They could see the house in the valley. He spoke about his vision for the land, the horses he wanted.

Shelby fell asleep. When she awoke, Gabe was on his back sound asleep. She studied his face, his nose, his chin. Gabe woke and sat straight up. He smiled at Shelby, cupped her face with his hands, and just stared. Shelby started crying. His fingers gently wiped her tears away.

They both seemed to be thinking the same thing. How awkward was the timing of this love! If they both didn't have such strong dreams they could be together, but without those dreams they would have never met. They held each other for a long time, then took another hike before heading home. He took her to the most beautiful landscape of Montana, but Shelby couldn't remember any of it. She laid her head on his shoulder and held tightly to his arm as they drove home.

The next few days went by quickly. Far too soon came the day when Mildred and Shelby were taking Gabe to the airport. Gabe offered to stay. Mildred knew that when it was time for Gabe to come home he would and that doing so before it was time wouldn't have been wise. Having Gabe there would have been a temporary fix for Mildred. She was going to have to face living in a home without Holt.

Shelby is standing in the living room, staring out the window as the rain came pouring down. She could her Mildred talking as Gabe was packing his last bag. He had asked Shelby only once. It had been about two in the morning. They were in the barn, backs against a wool blanket to protect them from the hay poking through the bales. The window on the upper loft was open and they watched the stars. He knew about the book, the project, the expectations; he understood. He proceeded anyway. "You could come with me," he said. "I love you. Come with me. Marry me." It wasn't a question but a statement.

She watched him board the plane. He didn't look back. The next day she left. Shelby let Mildred hold her after she put the last suitcase in place.

She arrived at Shelby Inn around seven that night. She wondered what Mildred was doing her first night without Holt or Gabe. She wanted to bolt back there and comfort Mildred, rescue her, or maybe it was she who wanted to be rescued? She took a bath, and went to bed. She slept late into the next day.

Shelby took the photograph out of her suitcase. For the first time since Mildred had given it to her, she looked at the picture. It was one of the many that had graced the long hallway. Mildred didn't know it had been the one Shelby liked the best. It had been raining and he had a yellow slicker on and was squatting down on some rocks and looking up with an incredible smile. She kissed it and then put it back in her suitcase, feeling foolish, like a teenager, kissing the picture of the quarterback in the yearbook.

In the passing months, Shelby would hear from Mildred every once in a while. She wondered if Gabe knew his mother was passing on the letters that Gabe had written her. They came from all over the world. Shelby kept every one of them.

One cold winter day she received a letter from Gabe. It contained Mildred's obituary and a short itinerary of Gabe's next three years, going as far away as Yemen. He had enclosed two gifts, a knotted leather bracelet, a tribal gift he had received and a compass, a gift Holt had received from Mildred before he had left for the war, so many years ago. On the back was inscribed, "You will always find your way back to me. Love, Mildred."

She read the paper and slowly sipped her tea. She was glad it was Saturday. It had been a long, hard week. Many small problems at the paper had kept her there late every night that week. There was a knock at the door. As she stood up, her sleeve caught the rough edge of the table. In a flash, she saw her life going by, remembering, seeing herself here at this same table, eating every high school dinner with Aunt Ellie, going on the road for years, the success of the project, Aunt Ellie's funeral, going back to work at the paper, never hearing from Gabe. Shelby caught a glimpse of herself in the hall mirror as she walked toward the front door.

She steadied the cup of tea on the saucer and wondered why she hadn't just set the cup down on the table. She noticed how old her hands looked next to the emerald ring, remembering how she had gone out and spent too much money on the ring. She had fallen in love with it and decided it was a consolation gift. She bought it two days after she had turned down the opportunity to write a second book and to do another traveling project. It was the only piece of jewelry she had ever bought herself. It looked gaudy next to the knotted leather bracelet. She smoothed her hair and swept a crumb from her clothes.

She opened the door, steadying the cup against the saucer. Slowly, the cup slipped from her hands. She heard it shatter on the hardwood floor. Shelby felt the pain as one of the pieces cut into the top of her left foot and she watched the saucer drop to the floor. Shelby took a deep breath as her eyes, for the first time in years, looked straight into those of Gabe Bradford.

The Salt Paper Letters

"**G**ET UP THERE!" Jamon whispers in a deep, raspy voice as he roughly pushes the boy forward. Jamon sneers as he smirks to his friend, "Those white folks love little dark beggars."

Fru slowly makes his way to the line. The line is long and Fru is too short to see too much in front of him. He hopes that this group of missionaries will have not only Bibles to give out, but also food. He is doubtful, since he can't smell or see any. He tries not to be disappointed.

Fru's stomach growls profusely reminding him it has been two or three days since he last ate. He smiles as he takes the Bible from a white woman. He doesn't want to leave. He wants to beg her to take him home with her. He wants to have a mother cook him meals and make sure he washes his face, someone who will smile at him right before he closes his eyes to sleep. On one side of the line where they were passing out Bibles, a white man is talking on a platform. He holds a Bible in his hand. An old, thin man stands next to the white man, interpreting in the people's language what he is saying.

He wants to cry but his father would not be happy to see his son cry. So, with a Bible in his hand, Fru makes his way back to his father. Jamon grabs the Bible from Fru and smacks him hard on the back. This is his father's way of showing his approval. His toothless father pushes his way through the crowd, the Bible tucked inside his shirt. Fru has to run to stay caught up. It is hard though, because he is thirsty and his stomach hurts.

Back home Fru sits silently and watches his father slowly tear out pages from the Bible. Jamon meticulously measures out salt for each page then closes it and binds it with string. Fru isn't sure what a Bible is, but there are many people who stand in line for them. Did they all take them home and put salt in them? In the days that would follow, they would walk from village to village until all the salt was sold.

His father would never tell him what the words said in the Bible. It was written in English and his father said English words weren't important. Fru knew they must be important if white people came from far away to deliver them. Fru hadn't seen many white people in his life, only missionaries, doctors and nurses who came to the village sometime. One time a scientist came. He studied the soil, talked to some people about water or something, but he never came back. Fru is getting sleepy, closes his eyes, and listens as his dad continues to measure and tie.

Fru's dad comes into their small hut and throws two pieces of fruit at him. Fru is told to eat slowly. Fru doesn't need to be told. He knows how long it can be between meals. He leans back on the chair and smiles. He can remember one week, in which every day they had gotten to eat. They had rice and some sort of beans and lots of corn. He went to bed smiling every night that week, every night happy and full. Fru sets the chair down on all four legs. That had been a long time ago.

In another village, Melelia slowly tends to her garden. She pulls a few weeds and then looks down the road as she has done for several days now, looking for Somnee, her husband, to return. Their small cupboard is almost bare and he is bringing food. That is the only reason she wishes for his return.

In the last few days, she has limited herself to only a piece of fruit a day. Yesterday, she ate two. After she had eaten one piece, she discovered a piece that looked as if it was going to rot and she knew that she could not waste it. She is also feeling very weak. She hopes her cabbage and beans will be ready to pick in a week or so.

The sun is setting and her workday is ending. She looks up to the sky and repeats her prayer as she has done for years. "Sky painter, your work is magnificent!"

Almost two weeks pass before Somnee returns. She is eager to see what he has bought but knows not to show it. She goes through one sack, finds what she needs and prepares dinner. She decides to go through the other sack tomorrow. It will give her something to look forward to.

The next day she is up early. She is very quiet as her husband sleeps. She takes the other sack outside. She gets to the salt and realizes that there are words on the paper. She is curious about the words she believes to be English. She doesn't know how to read English but her sister will know. Veresha knows how to read English very well.

Melelia will have to get her husband's permission to go. It is a two–day walk and she wants to be back in time to tend her garden. Her husband is good about looking after it but sometimes he eats things before the crop is ready and then they have less throughout the season.

Her husband most of the time is happy to see her go. Veresha always sends back a couple of small coins and candy for him. Veresha and her husband have much more wealth than she and Somnee.

Her sister is delighted to see her and greets her with hugs and a deep kiss on the cheek. It is not their custom to touch, but it was different for them. They didn't care, they loved each other. Visits among woman and relatives are rare and they miss each other terribly.

It is late and dark, so they go to bed. They have to rise early tomorrow and work in the fields. Melelia tries to fall asleep but she can't, although she aches from the long walk and is very tired. The beads that separate this small room from the other bedroom moves. It is Veresha, and just as when they were little, they sleep in the same small bed. Before falling asleep, they pat each other's head three times. When they were little, it had been a game they played when it was late at night and they couldn't talk. Two long pats meant "all okay." Two short pats were "always friends," three pats for "I love you."

They both wake before sunrise, quietly leaving the house. They walk down the road to the fields. They don't talk much. Just being together is the most important thing for them.

When it is light outside, Melelia nervously takes the paper out of her pocket. As her sister begins to read, she wants to weep but continues to listen intently. Verisha has to read it three times before Melelia lets her quit. The top corner says Psalms, Psalms 36:5-11, Thy loving kindness, O Lord, extends to the heavens, Thy faithfulness reaches to the skies. Thy righteousness is like the mountains of God. Thy judgments are like a great deep. O Lord, Thou preservest man and beast. How precious is Thy loving kindness O God and the children of men take refuge in the shadow of Thy wings. They drink their fill of the abundance of Thy house and Thou dost give them to drink of the river of Thy delights. For with Thee is the fountain of life. In Thy light we see light. O continue Thy loving kindness to those who know Thee and Thy righteousness to the upright in heart. Let not the foot of pride come upon me and let not the hand of the wicked drive me away. (KJV)

Melelia asks to hear it one more time before her sister insists they get to work. During the day as they work the fields, Verisha teaches Melelia bits and pieces of English.

They talk quietly, as they know if they are caught even knowing English, let alone teaching it to other women, there will be a high price to pay.

On her walk home, she studies the paper. On the second day of her journey, the sun is setting and she is looking for a place to lay her head. Once again, she thanks the sky painter for the sunset when she hears loud voices of men. Her heart is beating rapidly as she hides behind a tree. They stop, not ten feet away from her. They are only using the bathroom and soon make their way down the road. It takes awhile but she finally falls asleep. The next morning she finds a few coins the men had dropped the night before. Melelia is very happy.

Fru sits in the corner of the dark hut and slowly sucks on a potato. He isn't ready to eat it, because too soon it will be gone. He chews on the peel until there is nothing left, it seems, and swallows.

Almost a year has passed when more white folks come to his village. It is more white folks with Bibles, but instead of staying one day, they are staying a whole week. They are preaching at night and holding a Bible school during the day. He can't wait. He is going to Bible school. He doesn't even know what that means. He has heard they serve fruit and rice everyday—the only reason he is allowed to go, says his father.

He loves these people. They help him with his English. They give him food and water–clean water–not the water he is used to drinking. On the last day, they give him a Bible. Later he learns it is the New Testament.

He can see his father sitting outside the hut. He ducks behind a tree. His father must not see the Bible, so Fru digs a hole in the dirt and covers it up. If his father sees the Bible, he will want to tear apart the pages and wrap salt in it.

In the middle of the night, rain wakes Fru. He gets out of bed and quietly tiptoes out of the house. He doesn't want his Bible to get wet. Although he is scared, he tucks it into his pants and heads back to his bed. He decides to bring it into the house. As he is coming back in, his father is awake and demands to know what he is doing. He drops the Bible. Was he running away? Was he stealing? He is beaten for his silence. He tries to pray as he was taught at Bible school.

A few years pass. Melelia yearns for more. She learns more of the sky painter's letters. A man named Paul, whose life seemed as difficult as hers. She knows something of a Jonah, but just like Paul's story, she isn't sure of what a sea is. And so days turn into weeks, weeks turn into months, the months turn into years. She has lost her husband and her sister. The few salt paper letters have worn thin through the years, making them hard to read, although she has memorized most of it anyway. She knows there is more.

It has been only three days since her son left. She hears his voice and throws down her hoe. Melelia wonders what would bring him back so soon. She wipes her hands on her apron as she runs down the road. She stubs her toe on a sharp rock and it begins to bleed. Although the dirt is seeping in, she ignores it.

Her son holds a Bible in his hands, a whole Bible. She doesn't know what he means. But then he shows her Psalms. The Psalms just like the page that she had shown him many years ago. They dance in the road. Her son departs early the next morning. She doesn't look at the Bible much. It is fall, harvest time, and there is much to be done.

It is now winter and she reads. Frustrated, she realizes her English is still not very good. Her son has tried to teach her, just like her sister tried. She realizes she is a slow learner, but she continues steadfastly. She reads about Jonah and all of the Psalms. She reads of Paul's journeys. She reads and reads. It all comes together. All these years, with just pages here and there. Now she has them all. She underlines the words she doesn't know, hoping that one day she will find someone to explain them.

Winter is almost over as the days are getting warmer. On a sunny day in March, Melelia has a foolish idea. A foolish idea some would say. If Paul could do it, so can she.

Two weeks later, Melelia wraps her few belongings in a small blanket, tying a rope around the worn blanket and fastening it to her waist. The worn thin scarf she ties around her head. Even though she is old, her heart feels young. She looks around, and straightens the small bowl that sits on the small wooden table. In the bowl is a letter for her son. She fastens the gate to the garden and begins walking.

Two months into her journey, she meets up with a boy. Not a boy really, a strong man, but everyone looks young to her. Melelia has found a kindred heart, someone whose mission is the same as hers.

And so as it was Fru and Melelia spend their days going from village to village, being the salt of the earth.